WARNING

This book contains sexually explicit scenes and adult language. It may be considered offensive to some readers. This book is for sale to adults ONLY.

* * * * * * * * * * * * * * * * * * *

Please store your files wisely where they cannot be accessed by underage readers.

ISBN-13: 978-1988083902
ISBN-10: 1988083907

Other Books by Darla Dunbar:

<u>The Romeo Alpha BBW Paranormal Shifter Romance Series</u> (This series precedes the "<u>Romeo Alpha Blood Lines Romance Series</u>")

Amanda Walker thinks that she has a normal and boring life. That is until after her 24th birthday. Everything changes when she meets the man who says he was supposed to be her husband. Denying everything the man says, she fights him every step of the way. But after he kidnaps her, Amanda discovers that there are some things about her family that her parents kept a secret all these years. Among the history of the family she learns secrets she thought only happened in story books. Can Amanda tell the difference between truth and lies or is she this mysterious woman that holds the key to a legacy?

<u>The Alpha Feud BBW Paranormal Shifter Romance Series</u>

Eliza's life consisted of reporting on boring, crowd-pleasing events, like their country livestock fair. With the arrival of two handsome brothers, the lives of Eliza and her best friend, Melissa, are shaken to the core. For Eliza, the arrival of this new man becomes a test of her relationship with her current boyfriend, who she's been happily living with for over six years. Does Hayden, a complete stranger, really wield the power to make Eliza reconsider her relationship with Andrew?

The Alpha Packed BBW Paranormal Shifter Romance Series

Darlene has led a quiet life since suffering through a terrible break-up. She wants nothing more than to spend her time in front of the TV, away from any sort of trouble. But all that goes down the drain when handsome, rugged and rough Idris comes into her life. He is a werewolf on the lookout for his missing pack leader. Darlene quickly finds herself pulled towards this mysterious man and at the same time finds herself falling deeper and deeper into the world of the supernatural.

The Daemon Paranormal Romance Chronicles

The daemon infighting can only be stopped when a strong leader emerges to calm the different factions. Juno appears to be at the heart of the conflict. Things become complicated when Phoebe and Supay try to negotiate with the siren, Juno. The love triangle among Phoebe, Supay and Apollo become tense when Juno's meddling threatens to destroy any romance that develops.

The Mind Talker Paranormal Romance Series

Ananda finds herself on the run and she's not alone. With help from Jared, a stranger that she just met, the two evade capture by an organization that is intent on hunting her kind. Ananda and Jared are able to read minds. When an unfortunate incident happened involving a disturbed individual that resulted in the death of his schoolmates, the secret organization decided to take action.

The Leather Satchel Paranormal Romance Series

Valtina is stuck in Middle World, unable to pass on to The Afterlife. In order to redeem herself from past deeds done, she must help bring romance back into the world and stop The Dark Side from destroying love in its entirety. Following orders issued by Ladaya and armed with a leather satchel filled with the appropriate tools and weapons, Valtina embraces each mission with enthusiasm.

Get the latest update on new releases from the author at:

https://darladunbar.com/newsletter/

This book is Part Three of the "<u>Romeo Alpha Blood Lines Romance Series</u>" and follows twenty-four years after "<u>The Romeo Alpha BBW Paranormal Shifter Romance Series</u>"

1 - Blood Lines

Twenty-four years have passed in relative peace for Amanda and Romeo. They've raised five children into adulthood and are thoroughly enjoying their lives as the Alpha King and Queen of the werewolves. At twenty-four, Sarina is just stepping into her powers and will be ripe for mating when her birthday comes in two weeks. What no one knows is the danger that lurks just outside their tight knit community. Romeo has made peace with the other clans and has enjoyed that peace, but it will all come crashing down around him when his oldest daughter comes of age to take a mate.

2 - Alpha Infiltration

Brody is an attentive and loving mate and Sarina finds herself engulfed by the love of her family. When things start to change with the twins though, Sarina finds herself torn in two. She loves Brody in a way she's never loved another man, human or wolf. When he shows signs of the dark void, however, she can't decide whether to run from him or to him. She's frightened for both of her sons and struggles with her own mortality.

3 - Alpha Bait

Lilith is on the loose, plotting and planning with Fenris to take down the Delta pack and its alpha, Romeo. Sarina and Brody have their work cut out for them in order to stop the hostile takeover. With their wedding on the horizon, both feel compelled to spend time with their family even as danger lurks around every corner. When the twin babies, Jedidiah and Brody Jr., go missing, all hands are on deck to search for the leaders of the next generation of the Delta pack. And as Sarina and Brody dig deeper into Lilith's past, especially where Romeo is concerned, they find a mind twisted by deception and an overly unhealthy obsession with power.

4 - Alpha Strategy

With Lilith's soul separated from her body, Romeo and Amanda are bent on seeing her body destroyed so that she never comes back again. What they've forgotten in the meantime is that Lilith wasn't alone in her desire over control of the Delta pack and Romeo. Sarina and Brody are finally enjoying a quiet life, not that they expect it to last long. Their wedding, a source of great stress, is just weeks away. With all that's going on though, Sarina wonders if she'll ever be able to legally wed her mate.

5 - Alpha Revelation

Lilith has haunted the Traverse family since the beginning but her obsession with the reigning alpha and his immediate family is more than Romeo's eldest daughter can stand. In a twisted allegiance with her first mate, Fenris, Lilith has caused unbearable pain to the Delta pack's community and now she has gone as far as to make a deal with the Devil. She has comfortably inhabited Sarina's body, playing wife to Brody and mother to the couple's twin boys. Digging her way up from Hell wasn't easy, but Sarina harnesses powers that rival even those of her mother.

Alpha Romeo Blood Lines Romance Series

Alpha Bait

Book Three

By Darla Dunbar

Table of Contents

Chapter One

SARINA TRAVERSE sat in her mother's living room perusing wedding magazines. As the oldest of the Walker-Traverse children, she felt a certain responsibility to throw a party no one would forget for some time to come. At least until Shawna married. The boys, Wade and Joshua wouldn't care one way or another when it was their turn to marry. Sucking in her lip she tried to stem the tears that still wanted to fall at the thought of her twin, Jason.

It had been nearly three months since he'd been killed by Lilith, the once dead and now reliving creator of the werewolf and initial maker of both of Fenris' packs. The Delta pack had risen, thanks in huge part to the Traverse clan, all the way back past Sarina's grandfather, Jeremiah. Romeo, Sarina's father, had worked hard, struggled and sacrificed to keep a peace between the Delta pack and other outlying packs. Some had even submitted their alpha position and joined themselves with the Delta pack, becoming a large family of werewolves who looked out for one another.

Sarina had been so excited to turn twenty-four, to do her part in keeping the Delta pack strong. Then she'd met her now mate, Brody. He was the father of her twin boys, Jedidiah and Brody Jr., who were just about to start walking and were already well on their way to forming sentences. Apparently growing quickly wasn't just a phenomenon that affected them in the womb, but for the whole of their lives, at least until the change came. She was grateful she had another ten to twelve years before that happened.

"He would have loved seeing them," Sarina said, her heart still broken. "Jason would have been the best uncle."

"Yes he would have," Amanda Traverse said softly. Since losing her son, Amanda had barely spoken. The first weeks after his death, she'd barely eaten enough to stay alive, so lost in her grief that she truly didn't care at the time whether or not she lived. Now, while she still wasn't herself, probably never truly would be again, she at least ate and conversed some. "Judging by his first change, you'd have a disgruntled opinion of your brother as uncle material. Jason was a little hellion during his first shift. Couldn't blame him though, it's a painful and overwhelming process."

"Sort of like our first breeding, huh?" said Sarina.

"A lot like it yes, but different, in so many ways. Our shift comes because we want it to. Our men shift whether they want to or not. Every full moon, they morph into werewolves and stalk into the brush and woods to find prey. Don't forget, my daughter. No one asks for this life. I found out at twenty-four what my parents were, who I was. It took me several more years to truly come to grips with the reality of it. Even after I'd married your father and had you and Jason."

"Was it difficult, learning all of that literally overnight?"

She knew she'd heard the stories a million times since she was little, but listening to them always soothed her soul and Sarina hoped they'd take her mother to a happier time. Anything to pull her from the loss of one of her children.

"Your father was like a handsome ogre. He was an overbearing ass who thought everything was his way or the highway. I just had to show him that compromise was definitely in his best interest." Sarina caught the hint of a smile on her mother's lips before her eyes dulled again. Moving closer, Sarina wrapped her arms around her mother, pulling her close.

"Tell me more?"

Amanda hugged her back. "It didn't take long for me to realize that I'd fallen head over heels for your father, not that he'd have had it any other way, peeping Tom. Still, I wasn't about to make it easy on him. I fought him tooth and nail for every inch of freedom. I stepped into the cabin Wade has now and your father acted as if I was the Holy Grail. Wouldn't let me have a moment's peace and quiet. After we found out that you and Jason were coming it was worse, except that I was halfway around the world. I couldn't reach your father at all and he was being tortured by Remus, your Aunt Audri's first love. Things got really complicated when my half-brother Dean came into the picture, trying to steal the Radiant powers my mother had given me. That's when I met your Aunt Penelope. She was so timid. I learned early in those first conversations that this was more to ensure her safety and the secret she kept, than her actual personality.”

“Aunt Pen sure has come into her own, hasn’t she?”

“That she has. I, of course, fully credit her and Elijah finding their own happiness. They could have torched a house with the sparks they gave off in the beginning, even when they didn’t think they could have a life together.”

“Why didn’t Aunt Pen just say *screw it* and become Uncle Elijah’s mate anyway?”

“Because while she loved him, she loved being a Radiant, the powers her mother passed to her. She wanted to honor them to the best of her ability and she didn’t think she could have both her powers and Elijah at the time.”

“She’s got more in her than I do,” Sarina said, looking out the window.

“Your aunt would tell you that it was because she loved Elijah that she didn’t throw it all away. She loved him enough to walk away from him, to let him move on, when she couldn’t have him and be a Radiant. As women, particularly mothers, we have to remember that sacrificing for our families doesn’t mean we give up the things we need. Your Aunt does a great job of balancing her needs and wants with those of her husband and child.”

“Planning this whole thing feels sort of strange.”

"Not all mates legally wed, you know?"

"I know, but after all that's happened this last year, I think both Brody and I need this. We need to know that come hell or high water, we will always choose each other, first and last. We've talked about it and in the beginning I think we sort of leaned towards not doing it, but there has been so much trying to weigh us down that we need a moment to step back, to thank everyone who's stood by and behind us in support. To say 'thank you' to everyone who's kept us safe. And who've worked to keep the boys safe."

"Any member of our pack would gladly give their lives to keep Brody Jr. and Jedidiah safe, you know that. Still, a wedding is a great way to get everyone together."

Sarina could tell that her mother was trying to be cheerful, trying hard not to let her grief show, trying hard and failing miserably at it. Still, she hoped helping with the wedding would bring a genuine smile to her face. "Why don't we plan a shopping trip?"

"Where?" asked Amanda.

"I don't know. Somewhere outside the pack. We never go outside anymore and nothing against the Delta, but we're a little behind the times and if I want a dress that's going to knock Brody off his feet, I need to look around."

"Your father isn't going to like it."

"Dad never likes anything. We're grown women. Plus, we can take Dad and Brody with us if they want to come. They can get some male bonding in over beer and pool, while we enjoy giggling like idiots over lace and tulle."

"Alright," Amanda said, the grief lifting from her eyes for a moment. "Maybe Jas…" Sarina caught the first sob from her mother before teary eyes met hers. Then her mother just turned and walked away. Her own grief was still very raw and Sarina found herself crying. She needed her twin, now more than ever. Who would be there to look after her boys when they no longer wanted their parents around? Who would teach them all the things she told them not to do? Wiping her eyes, she sniffled before she stepped out of the living room straight into her little brother, Wade. Barely more than a year behind her and Jason, he favored their father just as much as she did their mother. "Hey," he said, his voice soft, understanding. "You okay?"

"Just grieving," she said, a sheepish smile curving her lips. "How about you?"

"The same," he grinned. "Just in a different way."

"Does it help with the grief?"

"Some, but I'm not sure Brody would like you doing it."

"What is it?" asked Sarina.

"Manual labor," he said. "Actually, I'm tracking the bitch who killed Jason. No luck so far, but I'm getting closer. I can feel it."

"That whore won't know what's coming when I get my claws and teeth into her. I'll rip her throat out before she can whimper," said Sarina.

"Now there's my sister," Wade smiled. "So, if you wanna help, just let me know. I'll be heading back out in about two hours."

"Hell yes," Sarina said.

"Good. The more wolves I have looking, the sooner I'll find her trail. Do you… do you think you can show me where he… where Jason was killed?"

"Yes," Sarina said without hesitation. If it helped Wade track that spineless wench, she'd do whatever it took to avenge her brother's death. Wade looked almost relieved.

"I hate asking you, Sarina."

"I'm offering," she replied, hugging her little brother. "Besides, my helping you kick that bitch's teeth down her throat might feel a little bit like justice for Jason. Lord knows we won't be getting it any other way."

Chapter Two

Sarina was ready to go when Wade came downstairs to grab a sandwich. She hadn't been able to convince Brody that she'd be fine with her brothers, so he'd brought the twins, Jedidiah and Brody Jr., over for Amanda to watch. They seemed to be the only bright spot in her life as she grieved the loss of her son.

"Be safe," Sarina heard her mother say. She stood off just a bit, holding a boy on each hip, her eyes showing her concern.

"We'll keep each other safe, Mama," Sarina promised. She kissed her mother's cheek and each little boy's forehead before she rejoined her mate and siblings.

"Wait!" she heard a rough, loud voice say. Sarina turned to see her father, Romeo Traverse, standing in the archway that led to the kitchen. "You'll not leave this house until I'm ready to go with you. That hell-bitch murdered my son and the rightful heir to this pack. She'll pay for her transgression by my hands."

No one said a word as they waited. Sarina had never seen her father so cold and callous. She hoped it was only because they were about to start a hunt for one of the most evil instigators of their kind anyone knew.

Sarina knew very little about Lilith. She knew that before she was born, Lilith had gone by the name Elena and that she'd been intimately involved with her father's twin, Damon. Apparently, from stories she'd heard, her father had seen the evil in her heart and killed her. Damon, as she'd expect, was furious and isolated himself from his family for years. He didn't surface again until Romeo found his own true love, Amanda. Damon kidnapped Amanda in hopes of seeking his revenge for the death of Elena. No one knew until much later that Elena hadn't died and that she was, in fact, Lilith. She'd been biding her time, pretending to be a halfwit assistant to Dean, Amanda's half-brother, all the while keeping her true identity disguised.

After Amanda and the other Radiants used their powers to defeat Dean, Lilith revealed her true self, claiming to have always been in love with Romeo and making bold claims of ownership over him. Eventually her father and mother, along with the other Radiants were able to kill Lilith. How that wench came to be back among the living, Sarina didn't know and while she wasn't exactly sure she wanted to find out, she wasn't about to let her hurt anyone else in her family. Losing Jason had greatly affected them all, especially Amanda. And Sarina knew she'd do whatever it took to bring her brother justice and restore the smile to her mother's face. If it was all she got out of Lilith's death, it'd be enough.

They made it to the place where Jason had been murdered, in less than two hours. Romeo ordered everyone to search for her trail while Sarina and Brody told both him and Wade exactly what had transpired. "Brody was in a trance for a while, as if Lilith had some sort of grip or spell on him. Then she just appeared in this blood red dress, looking like a seductress. She leapt onto Jason as if he were primed for sex," Sarina blushed. It wasn't normal for her to discuss such intimate topics, especially with her father and brother. "The more I tried to reach him, the more she clung to him, whispering her lies into his ear. I tried to help him get free from her and that's when she tossed me against the tree as if I weighed nothing. She had me by the throat with one hand and when Jason came at her, having changed into his wolf; she simply caught him in mid-leap and broke his neck."

"Which tree was it, the tree you hit?"

Sarina looked around the area, closing her eyes to focus. She recalled the events with vivid clarity, her heart breaking as she remembered her twin coming to her rescue only to be cut down in the prime of his life. Then her pretty green eyes opened and she walked over to a tree and rubbed it with her hand. "This one. This is where she threw me."

Without so much as a warning, Romeo changed and sniffed the ground for her scent. He walked back and forth, nosed leaves out of his way, sniffed again. Then, just when she thought he'd change back and she'd have to let him borrow her jacket, he sat down, lifted his head and howled. The sound was the heart-wrenching sound of a man who now knew the musky scent of his child's killer. "Lead us on, Romeo," Brody said, grabbing Sarina's hand.

They followed Lilith's scent for miles, reaching a huge clearing far east of the caves where Sarina had been rescued shortly after delivering her twins. Sarina saw her father's eyes as he stopped and sat down. He couldn't exactly talk to her, but she understood he wanted her to wait while he went forward alone. She didn't like the idea, but she nodded her head in understanding. She reached forward and ran a hand down his back and smiled when his tongue licked her hand. "Be careful," she said as he headed out at a soft trot.

Sarina found a place on the edge of the forest where she and Brody sat to wait. She leaned into him, thankful for his strength. They'd been through so much since the twins' birth that she often felt they barely knew each other now. Lifting her head, she pressed her lips to his and felt the heat flash through her body. His hand played with her long, dark hair, tugging it playfully. When she opened to him, he gladly took them deeper, eliciting a soft moan from her. "I've missed you," she said, a soft smile on her lips.

"I've missed you too," he said, pressing his brow to hers.

Sarina settled against his chest again, feeling his arm wrap around her. She nodded off, knowing her father would be a while yet.

Sarina woke later to excruciating pain, her head felt as if someone had pulled all her hair out by the roots. When she looked around though, the sight before her chilled her blood. The wolves that had accompanied her, and Brody lay dead, slaughtered like lambs at the butcher. "What do you think?" came a cackling little laugh. Sarina turned to see Lilith in a gold gown that left little to the imagination. "I did it as a present for your father."

"My father is repulsed by you. Do you really think he'll come to you when you murdered his son?"

"Oh, doll," she laughed. "He'll not only come to me, he'll beg me to mate with him. Don't you know how it was between us?"

"I know you had some ridiculous fascination with him. Apparently you haven't learned to move on. Slow-witted, aren't you?" Sarina yelped when sharp nails raked across her face, scoring her cheeks with deep incisions.

"Watch your tongue, you worthless spawn."

"You don't own me, you bitch!" Sarina yelled through the pain searing her face. Anger and grief mixed a dangerous potion in her heart as she reached out to deal her own amount of damage. When her hand passed through what would have been Lilith's middle, Sarina quickly pulled her hand back.

Lilith just stood there laughing. "You naïve little whelp. You know nothing of the power I wield. Why don't you go home and leave what's between your father and me for us to settle ourselves? You always were second best you know. Had I not been so impatient and angry, I would have used your brother's body for so much more. A waste really. But it did bring your father here, so I suppose killing his spawn, one of them at least, wasn't as impulsive as I thought."

Sarina held in her anger. She knew now that the woman before her was an illusion at best. She'd need to study to know if hurting her was possible when she was nothing but vapor. Even so, she couldn't wait to get a piece of her. "I have no doubt that my father will tear you limb from limb when he gets his hands on you. I hope he peels your skin off of you while your flesh bakes in the sun. You're a black plague to our kind and it's obvious, even if not to you, that you need to be eliminated."

The laugh was back, grating on Sarina's ears. "I can't wait to see you try, you spineless little whore." Just when Sarina was about to give attacking her another try, she woke with a start, her body still cuddled next to Brody. She shook him hard, startling him from his own sleep. Collapsing against him, she sighed before telling him what happened. She rambled so fast that the whole story was out before he was able to get through to her.

"Sarina, she scratched you."

"What?" Sarina asked, pressing her hand to her cheek and wincing in pain. "How in the hell? Brody, she was like an apparition. I tried to attack her and my hands went right through her as if she were a mist. Whatever witchcraft she's using, it's pitch black and dangerous."

"Will your mother be able to handle it?"

"I don't know, but we need to find my dad and get back to my mother. We need the Radiants, all four of them, and I need to talk to my dad."

An hour later Romeo showed up and listened to Sarina's story, showing anger at the deep slash on her face. "She'll pay for every one of her transgressions where my children are concerned," he said, his voice fatally serious.

Chapter Three

Lilith sat back on her bed and sighed. She'd shown that little piss-ant of Romeo's what she was capable of. Imagine the surprise that must have rushed through her when she'd tried to hurt her, only to find out Lilith wasn't really there. Oh she'd been real enough to scar that bitch's face, but how she loved the look on Sarina's face when her hands had gone right through her. Her laugh was full and rich as she enjoyed her little victory. If that didn't enrage Romeo, she didn't know what would. She'd expected almost immediate retaliation for Jason's murder and yet, today had been the first whiff of any searching she'd had. She couldn't wait to ravage his whole family and bring him whimpering to her bed. Her body already knew exactly what she wanted and when she made that little pussy her bitch, he'd do whatever she asked of him.

Lilith heard a knock at her door and sighed, closing her robe slightly. She liked the privacy of her own rooms. She liked walking around in the skin she'd been born to. It was a freeing experience and being interrupted only served to irritate her. "Come in," she commanded.

"I trust you had a pleasant time tormenting the Delta pack's leading little lady?"

Lilith looked at Fenris. She couldn't believe how much he'd aged since she'd been killed. It still galled her that Romeo and his little bitch queen had been able to manage it, but the past was the past after all. Fenris, as much as she hated to admit it, was her future, at least for now.

"I enjoyed myself quite a bit, if that's what you're asking."

"Excellent," he smiled. "Now, how about we figure out what to do going forward?"

"I'd love to talk war, but right now I'm trying to relax and having you in my space makes that difficult."

"We can't let this rest," Fenris argued. "We need to strike while their defenses are down."

"I couldn't agree more," she smiled. "Now, if you'll leave so I can rest and think, I'm sure I'll know where I'd like to go moving forward."

Fenris hated the way she dismissed him. As if he were just chattel to be sloughed off at her whim. Didn't she see his value? The way he'd set her up perfectly to get what she wanted? Didn't that deserve some acknowledgement?

"I'm afraid I can't do that," he said. He stood straighter, coming to his full height. It was an overtly obvious challenge to her and he found himself incredibly aroused when she stood up and her robe fell open, exposing her naked flesh. Her breasts were still gorgeous and her softly sloped belly speared down to a triangle of soft, silky curls that covered her most intimate place.

"You'll do as I say, Fenris. Do you not remember your making? Who it was that gave you the powers you have? I may have died, but as you can see I am very much alive now and I will not be challenged, not even by the likes of you."

Looking down at her, Fenris felt his cock bulge against the light fabric of his pants. Despite her wanderings and even her death, he still found it impossible to convince himself that he didn't want her. He brought his hands to her arms and was quickly brushed off. Irritated, he grabbed her again, firmer. He found himself flung against the wall and a grin played over his mouth. She wanted to fight and that only turned him on more.

"I'm not in the mood, Fenris. If you push me, you'll pay the price for your insolence."

"Please," Fenris grinned again. "I can already tell by the way your body moves that you just want to toy with me before I mount you."

"You always were an eager, playful lover. Your main problem is that you still think you're that young, attractive pup. You don't seem to grasp that you've aged and have become something far less desirable. Whether or not your libido is still intact hardly matters when I can barely bring myself to climax with you. You simply must find yourself a young bitch to meet your needs Fenris. There's nothing here for you."

"But you'll go to him," Fenris said, anger flashing through him. "You'll gladly spread your legs for that ass hat, Romeo."

"I'll spread my legs for my mate, yes. The issue I'm having is that he no longer remembers our mating, thanks to that cunt who took my place. At least in position. I know damn well she could never outdo me in bed, although letting her join us is always a possibility, when I've put her in her place. Witch or not, she can't hold a candle to my abilities. Once Romeo remembers our joining, our mating, he'll gladly come back to me and I'll spend weeks in sexual bliss. It's a fact you'll have to get used to."

"Then I want her," Fenris said, almost begging like a petulant child. "If you're going to turn me out and take him as your mate, then I want his current mate. She's young and beautiful."

"Fine," Lilith grinned. "Maybe we'll enjoy a foursome sometime, once everything gets back to normal."

"Make her docile," Fenris ordered. "I like a little spice sometimes, but not from her. I want her as docile as a newborn kitten."

"Kittens bite," she reminded him.

"Not this one," he said before turning to walk out.

He hated her sometimes. Other times he couldn't get her out of his head. With his body already worked up, Fenris stepped into the commune area where all the single wolves who had yet to mate hung out during the day. "Axis!" he called.

A pretty little blonde came over to him, her body built like a pixie. She was small featured, but Fenris knew she would accommodate him easily. He took her hand and without another word, led her to his quarters. "Strip," he ordered and sat back to watch her. She started to take her shirt off, dancing to some tuneless music in her head. As her body emerged from beneath her clothes, Fenris began to imagine what it'd be like with Amanda for their first time. Knowing she'd produced five healthy children, he knew he could be rough with her. He was all for a woman's first time as it was a sacred rite they needed, but sometimes the animal in him needed to run free and with Amanda he'd be able to do just that.

He smiled as he contemplated whether or not Romeo had ever taken her with a ruthlessness that Fenris could deliver. Sex was great and making love had its place for sure, but every once in a while, the wolves needed to screw, hard.

As soon as Axis was naked, Fenris pulled her to him. He pressed her against the wall beside his bed and bent down to taste her kiss. "I want to ravage you," he breathed. When her own breathing picked up and her leg wrapped around his, Fenris stripped his pants and boxers off. He came to her, his cock hard and ready. Running the tip of his hard shaft against the liquid heat of her pussy, Fenris filled her hard on that first thrust and pummeled her body, banging her so hard that her body bounced against the wall roughly with each press of his member. His rhythm was fast and ruthless as he plundered her body for his own needs. Using his hands, he roughly kneaded her breasts, squeezing their tips until she cried out. Continuing with her, Fenris picked her up and tossed her onto his mattress, giving himself an angle that would allow him to penetrate her deeper.

Her warm heat engulfed him, reminding him how sweet it was to have a woman at his disposal. Still, he wasn't as careless a lover as he wanted to be and sought her own orgasm as he did his own. Using his thumb, Fenris circled her clit, wetting it with her own, ripe juices. "Come for me, Axis," Fenris begged, his body on the verge of exploding. He felt her build quickly beneath him then and as her body fell off that rocky edge, Fenris pushed her over and followed her down as he pumped, spilling himself into her.

<<<>>>

Brody pressed a cold cloth to the swelling on Sarina's cheek. Amanda had done the stitching, but the welts had inflamed to an angry red against her porcelain skin. He was proud of the way she'd handled it all, taking it in stride. Her anger was well-controlled and would aid her well when they fought Lilith, a woman he now hated with as much passion as the entire Traverse clan. Jason's death had been hard on all of them, even him as he was just beginning to know his mate's twin as if he was his own brother. Now, she'd reached out and harmed what was his and he'd make sure, in line with everyone else, that Lilith paid dearly for her contravention.

"Keep that there, doctor's orders." Brody kissed her brow before his attention settled on the two boys who looked equally like him and Sarina. Brody Jr. was nearly the spitting image of his mother, dark hair, light green eyes, light skin. Jedidiah on the other hand was dark like his father with his light hair and blue eyes setting him up nicely to be a lady killer when he grew older.

"And if I don't?" Sarina grinned.

"Then I'll tie you down and make you keep it there."

"Promise?" she teased, finally feeling as if she and Brody had put the hard life of the last few weeks behind them.

"Absolutely," Brody smiled. Picking Brody Jr. up in one arm and Jedidiah in the other, he leaned over and gladly accepted Sarina's kiss, biting his tongue to keep from taking it farther. How long had it been since he'd touched her? Had he even been intimate with her since Lilith had finally released him? Closing his eyes as need slammed through his system like a freight train at full speed, Brody turned and toted the boys downstairs. "Keep that rag on for fifteen," he called back up to Sarina.

Later that night, when the boys were finally asleep, Brody tiptoed over to the room he shared with Sarina. He'd finished his work in his office and somehow during the day he'd managed to keep from taking her against a wall every time he saw her. Now though, when the house was quiet, his need wouldn't let him rest. "Hey," he said when he came into the room. Sarina was lying on her side, sound asleep. Brody sighed, knowing it'd be a long, silent night. He climbed into bed next to her and pulled her closer, her body folding into his. He forced his need away, closed his eyes, breathed her in, and sank into a deep, dreamless sleep.

<<<>>>

He woke up to the screaming sound of his name. He heard Sarina's hysterical voice coming from the twin's bedroom area. "Brody!"

"Sarina?" he asked, still waking from his sleep.

"They're gone," she said, her eyes wild, frightened. "The boys are gone. I've looked everywhere," she said.

"Have you called your parents?" he asked.

"No, I…I will," she finally said, seeming to calm down some. "It's that bitch!" Brody took a deep breath as his muscles clenched, ready for a fight. He followed Sarina to the phone and listened as she talked to her father.

"We'll be right there. Thanks, Daddy."

"What'd he say?"

"He's going to have Mama do a location spell for them. I'm just hoping this doesn't send her down further," she said, her eyes finally drying. They grabbed their coats and headed out with the blankets the boys used at night. It would help Amanda strengthen the location spell she'd use to find her grandsons.

Chapter Four

"Come to us this night. To aid our search for innocent hands. Wind, Earth, Fire and Water seek what is hidden and bring it to the light." Amanda touched the twins' blankets as her eyes went bright white. Sarina watched in awe, always touched by her mother's power. She'd once thought, as a little girl, that it'd be neat to have powers like her mother, but sitting here now, she realized the burden her mother carried. While she did so with much grace and humility, Sarina knew the gift wasn't meant for her. Her life was complicated enough as an alpha werewolf's daughter, especially now that her twins were missing.

Within minutes the spell was over and Amanda was coming back to herself. Sarina wanted to rush to her, to beg her for what she knew, but Sarina had learned long ago that her mother would only dispense the knowledge so that action could be taken as quickly as possible. "They're beyond our borders, towards the caves. Lilith only took them to get to you," she said, turning to look at Romeo.

"Does her obsession know no bounds, that she'd kidnap two innocent babies?"

"She'll kill for you," Amanda said, heatedly. "We both know that. Having you before was a test. Now she'll stop at nothing until you're hers."

"How do we kill her permanently? We killed her before and the bitch came back," said Romeo.

"We have to separate her soul from her body and destroy both. If her soul were to find a new body before we destroy it, she'd be able to come back again."

"And how do we do that?" asked Sarina.

"We beat her at her own game," Amanda said, looking straight into Sarina's eyes.

Sarina knew what was coming, but she didn't want to hear it. She knew, also that her mother didn't approach the subject lightly. "I'll do whatever you think is best, Mama," Sarina said, grabbing her mother's hand.

"We need to get started, today," Amanda said, seeming to gain the sense of purpose that she'd lost after Jason's death. "I'm going to contact Penelope, Briana, and Lucia. I'll need the help of their elements in order to make sure everything goes as planned."

"What exactly is the plan?" Romeo asked. Sarina looked at her father and for the first time saw how Jason's death had aged him. He was no longer the fun-loving father she remembered from her youth, but the hardened man who'd do whatever it took to protect his pack, his family.

Amanda spelled out the plan as best she could, leaving finer details for a later discussion once everyone had gathered. So far, she'd been right, Sarina didn't like it one bit. It meant leaving her sons in the hands of a crazy bitch who thought of nothing but what would aid her obsessive cause at getting Romeo Traverse to seek her out.

"I don't like it," she complained to Brody in her old room upstairs. "But I don't see any other way to end this. I won't let her kill any more members of our pack. Killing Jason nearly took both of my parents out. I can't imagine what will happen if we lose anyone else. Not to mention the families that lost loved ones on the preemptive attack Fenris pulled. We owe them something earth shattering for all they've cost us."

"I don't like it either," Brody agreed. "However, I've come to trust your parents and your mother's ability. If there's a way to get this psycho to die once and for all, we need to do our damnedest to make sure we succeed. Because, even when we get the twins back, if we don't kill her dead for certain this time, she'll continue to cause us trouble."

"I totally agree," Sarina said, letting Brody pull her into his embrace. It wasn't an easy thing, to sit idle when your children were in the hands of a crazy, sociopath. Sarina headed to the kitchen, hoping that preparing food would help her keep her mind from unraveling.

"Can I help?"

"Sure," Sarina said to her little sister, Shawna. With six years between them, Sarina had always thought of Shawna as a pest. Now though, as they'd both grown and matured, especially over the last couple of years, Sarina saw in her sister an asset she was blessed to have. "How are Mom and Dad handling everything?" asked Sarina.

"I'd say they're fine, but I'd be lying. Dad's angry and hard, something he's never been. Even after you found Brody, Dad wasn't this unapproachable. I think losing Jason really messed them up. Mom's lost herself somewhere. I'm hoping that working to find the twins and take out Lilith will help bring her back to herself."

"Maybe having Aunt Penelope, Briana and Lucia here will help."

"Let's hope so," Shawna agreed. The two women worked hard to make a dinner that would satisfy even their hunger for revenge. Each of them had a personal stake in finding the twins and seeing both Lilith and Fenris pay for their obvious mistakes. Romeo was a fair and just ruler, a leader that everyone in the Delta pack looked up to. It wasn't smart to cross him, especially where his family was concerned. The fact that Lilith didn't seem to care and was blatantly overstepping her bounds was a great concern.

"So," Romeo said, his eye meeting everyone at the table in turn. As far back as Sarina could remember when it came to dinner, they'd always eaten at the table as a family. In times of crisis or celebration it was the one place they always gathered, a place where one could always find a smile to share or tears to shed. "I need to know as much about her now as we can, everyone does. What she looks like now, weaknesses, if you noticed any other obsessions, etc. Anything you two can remember will help."

Sarina caught Brody's nervous stare before he spoke. "She, Lilith, exudes a sort of sexual aura. She uses it to her considerable advantage when dealing with men. I'm certain she used it on both myself and Jason before he was killed. When I was finally free of her in my mind, I was stunned even as I tried to reach Jason and Sarina. Forgive my crudeness, but Lilith threw herself at him as if he was the last candy bar within a million miles and she was having a hypoglycemic episode. I'm certain she knew he was your son and that Sarina was also your daughter. I don't think though," he hesitated before continuing, "that she wanted to kill him. She was all over him moments beforehand. I think she did it out of impulse, which would be a great disadvantage to her. She doesn't often think before she acts, at least that time she didn't."

"That's good," Romeo said. "Thank you."

"She's also extremely jealous of you and Mom," Sarina said. "She hates Mom and wants to take her place. She seems to think that by joining with you, she'll take her rightful place. Did you and Lilith have something, before Mom… before you mated?"

"What?" Romeo said, his voice bruising in its roughness. "How dare you—"

"She said you would remember who your real mate was and I took it to mean that she thought somewhere in her mind she must have thought that you two had mated sometime in the past."

"If she did, she's delusional as well, which would be another advantage," said Romeo, realizing the intent of Sarina's question.

"Could she have mistaken you for Uncle Damon?" Sarina asked. It wasn't common to bring up her father's brother, seeing as he'd died long ago and had never seen any of his twin's children. But Sarina thought it worth mentioning as it would make sense and could clear this whole thing up much easier than an all-out war, which was what Lilith seemed to be pushing for.

"No," Romeo said, shutting down her idea completely. "Before we killed her last time she said she'd never been in love with Damon and that she'd only been with him to get closer to me. Her single focus has always been me, unfortunately."

Sarina knew the idea brewing in her mind was ludicrous, but it was so strong that she voiced it before she could talk herself out of it. "What if we give her exactly what she wants?"

"What?"

"Hear me out," she said, rushing on. "Her single focus has always been getting to you. So what if we give her that? You'd be able to keep an eye on the twins and gain extremely valuable intel."

"So you think I should just waltz over to her, claim to love her, and let her dominate me?"

"No," Sarina said, impatient. "I think we should trick her into thinking that she's finally won you over. Then, when the time is right, we'll separate her from her body and destroy both her body and her soul, if you can call it that."

To her it didn't matter that everyone seemed to think she'd lost her mind. Her children were in danger, her brother had been murdered, her wedding day was pretty much ruined without Jason, and at least delayed because of this sordid wench; Sarina didn't know why everyone couldn't see the sense in her plan.

"I think she's right," Sarina heard her mother say, nearly dropping her fork in the process.

"You do?" Brody said, irritatingly so.

"I do," Amanda said again, more confidently. "And no, I don't say that lightly. It'll mean sending my mate, the man I've loved for more than half of my life, into a den of vipers. However, it's the only way I can see to keep little Brody Jr. and Jedidiah safe. Not to mention it'll give us a chance to figure out how to get that bitch out of her body and into hell where she belongs."

"I don't like it," Romeo sighed. "But I agree with Amanda. I don't see any other way to keep the boys safe. If we attack them outright, she'll kill them to spite us. Even if we try to out flank her, she'll kill them. Our best solution is to give her what she wants and to pray that we can defeat both Lilith and Fenris from the inside out."

Chapter Five

Romeo retreated to his chambers with Amanda. A long night of planning lay ahead of them and he needed the quiet to think. "You're worried," he said, when their doors were closed.

"Would you be happier if I pretended I wasn't? That whore killed our son, the one who was supposed to take over this pack. Now I'm going to send my husband in there, virtually unarmed against a centuries old whatever she is, who happens to be obsessed with you. You know she's going to want to sleep with you, right?"

"I've thought of that, yes. I'll have to hope that I'm smarter than she is. Perhaps you can give me something that will make me appear to be ill when I use it?"

Amanda huffed out a breath and turned toward the cupboard that housed her potions. She pulled out several vials and laid them on their bed. Fetching a label maker, Amanda ran off labels for the seven vials. "Each of these has a different purpose, which I'll put on the label. However, if you mix a drop of each of them together and drink the concoction, it'll make you smell so foul even she won't want to touch you. You can come up with the excuses however you like."

"I love you, Amanda," he said, reaching for her hands. They'd aged little over their nearly twenty-six years together. Amanda's hair was still the dark brown of a dark oak and her eyes still the bright, seafoam green he loved. Even after five children, her body was still splendid. Pulling her closer, he nuzzled her neck. "Be with me tonight. One more time before I step into her lair."

Her soft sigh vibrated against his neck, touching the scar she'd put on him so long ago, when she'd barely known who or what she was. Memories flashed through his mind of their first time together. She hadn't loved him then, hadn't even liked him really. But the tie between them was much too strong for either of them to deny. In the years since that first time, Romeo had learned to love her without the need to dominate and Amanda had learned to see the line between doing what was best versus doing what she wanted. All in all, they'd meshed very well since those first, very heated encounters.

Brushing his lips lightly over hers, he teased her. He roamed over her face and neck, using his hands to spread heat through her body. He grinned when her own hands did the same. They sought the warmth of his flesh as he worked to build the passion between them.

"Romeo," Amanda whispered, breathing against his skin as her lips pressed against his neck. Their days of making love recklessly throughout the house were long gone. With children still at home and grandchildren who'd soon be running around, there were only so many places they could comfortably express themselves, but Romeo had made sure to accommodate their closed in quarters by ensuring both their bed and bathroom were massive. Half of the upstairs had been redone when Amanda became the official owner. Their bathroom sported a custom built claw-foot tub, a separate two person shower with dual shower heads and two separately adjusting faucets. The first time they'd ever showered together and Amanda had complained about having to wait and running out of hot water, Romeo had made a mental note to do the bathroom up right for his mate. He'd made the wait worth it, revealing it as her wedding present. "It's still the best present I've ever been given," she smiled when he led her there.

"Really?" he said, thankful that she seemed willing. But now, Jason's death had scarred her in a way he'd never imagined and since then she'd been the hollowed out shell of the woman he'd fallen in love with. He knew her pain, had felt the majority of it himself. He didn't know what it was to carry a child inside him, but he knew what it was to hold them when they cried, to commit to raising them to be well-adjusted, loving, caring, kind, polite, useful adults. He knew the heart-wrenching pain of their loss, a loss no parent should feel. So, while he didn't know exactly what she'd felt, he knew most of it and empathized greatly with her. "I would have thought it'd be something more girly."

"No," she said, her green eyes glowing in the low light. "This, this wonderful labor of love is the best present you've ever given me. The children, they are on a separate level that doesn't connect to this one. Nothing can touch what they mean to me, but speaking of presents that you personally have given me, this is still my absolute favorite."

"Well in that case," Romeo smiled, pulling her closer. "I'm exceedingly glad I did it."

"Me too," she grinned. "Wanna try and see if we can run the hot water out?"

"Absolutely," he chuckled. "With two water heaters, though, I doubt we can last that long before our bodies shrivel up like prunes."

"Well, it'll be worth a shot, isn't it?"

"I'm right behind you."

Sarina stepped into her home nearly twenty-four hours after she'd left it. Neither she nor Brody said a word. She was emotionally exhausted, as she was sure he was. Without warning, she found herself pressed against the wall, Brody's mouth hotly claiming hers, like a starving man who'd found the choicest food. She gave into the need that clawed at her, the hunger she hadn't truly felt since the twin's birth. The full moon would rise that night and she knew Brody would change in a matter of hours. He'd hunt and tonight, she'd be by his side.

Now though, was the human need of their nature, just as strong and feral as the wolves that lived inside of them. Sarina grazed her teeth over his full lips, breathing heavily when he growled. His hands tore at her clothes, shredding them from her body with little care for where they landed or the outfit they ruined. His lips trailed hot, wet kisses over her skin, arousing her passion so that her mind couldn't think about anything, especially the two boys who were being left in the hands of a mad woman. "Brody," she said, breathing heavily before he picked her up. His dark eyes held her for a minute before he took her mouth again. The trip upstairs was quick and silent as Brody carried her to the guest room. By some silent agreement, they both knew that their room was off limits. It would remind them of their sons and now wasn't for that, not if they were going to do this whole thing right.

Sarina wasn't nearly as strong, even in her wolf, as Brody, but she still managed to strip him naked. She remembered all too well how it'd been for them two years earlier when they'd chosen to mate. That same, unruly passion still rocked so easily between them, despite all that had happened. She noted the way her hands shook when she reached out to touch him. His body was much the same while hers had changed irreversibly carrying the twins. Still, Brody seemed to love the way she looked, his body showed rather obvious signs of arousal.

It wasn't the norm between them for her to be the aggressor. She usually let him lead and enjoyed the ride, but tonight there was a need in her to have her way this time. Stepping closer to him, she boldly took his thick cock in her hand, stroking it slowly back and forth so that he had to close his eyes to control his need to ravage her. Her free hand traveled over the muscles of his chest, abdomen and arm, finally pressing against the muscles in his back to get him closer.

"Sarina," he begged, breathless. She'd known power over the years, especially since becoming a breeder. She knew women had an innate sense of dominance over their mates when it came to sex, specifically during their mating cycles, but just now, when she wasn't in heat, she wanted to express that power in a completely different way. Turning them, Sarina pressed Brody down onto the bed. She kissed his abs, working over his narrow hips and upper thighs. She teased him, drawing within a whisper of his hard cock and then drawing away to kiss the sensitive flesh of his inner thighs. Sarina did this until his hands buried themselves in her thick hair. Then she covered his tip with her lips, splashing him with a wet slide of her tongue. Brody's groan only encouraged her and she made her movements much more rhythmic, taking him deeper and deeper. His cock hit the back of her throat over and over again and Sarina fought the urge to gag, focusing on her movements so that his pleasure would bloom under her touch. His hands tugged at her hair as she continued to give him fellatio and soon Sarina found herself tasting the essence of his orgasm before she found herself under him. His hands worked to master her body, quickly drawing out her own arousal as his fingers sank into the wet heat between her thighs. She arched against him, his thumb wreaking havoc on her clit as he circled it over and over again. Aching for their joining, Sarina pulled him to her while moaning when he filled her with one hard thrust. Each penetration after that was deeper and harder than the last as Sarina felt her body being pushed toward completion. Brody's teeth clamped over her tight nipple, alternating between a teasing graze and a soothing flick of his warm tongue as he tortured her in the most intimate way.

Sarina could feel her body building beneath Brody's expert attention, her swollen pussy aching for each press of his hard cock. Over and over again he plunged into her, his deep thrusts pressing her closer to climax as his hands took the rest of her body over. The waves began like tsunamis, crashing through her as she clenched around him, tightly encasing him inside her wet, hot center. She cried his name as she came, feeling his own release as she pressed her hips tight to him, needing to feel him fully inside of her.

Over the last two years, Sarina had learned that Brody, while an amazing lover, wasn't one for cuddling after the fact. So when he pulled her close this time, she quickly relaxed against him, needing this moment just as desperately it seemed, as he did. "We needed this," he said, before she could speak.

"What do we do now?"

"We trust your parents," he said, something most men wouldn't. Brody, she knew, wasn't one to suggest something lightly, but Sarina couldn't help but wonder if it was because he was a once upon a time alpha who now submitted to her father, or if he truly thought her parents' plan would work. "And no, I don't particularly care for it."

"How did you know I—"

"We're linked, remember?" he said, nuzzling her neck. "I may not know exactly how you would have phrased it, but I knew you were wondering why I'd agreed to it."

"Not even my own thoughts are safe," she grumbled.

"Don't worry love," he grinned. "I'll keep your mind honest."

"What's that supposed to mean?"

"It means that women over analyze. Men are solution oriented. We're built to fix problems. Sometimes though, the only problem is that most women have trouble telling the lies in their head to *shut the hell up*."

"So you think I lie to myself?"

"I think everyone lies to themselves. In this instance, I think you were close. Look," Brody sighed. "I'm not saying that anyone, particularly you, does it on purpose. Self-lies are tricky, they sneak their way in without much provocation and before you know it, you're telling yourself all sorts of things that aren't true."

"Give me an example," she said.

"Alright," he smiled. "When Lilith was inside of me and things were strained between us, did you ever think to yourself that I was stepping out on you?"

"No," she said, but when those knowing, dark eyes met hers, she couldn't help but grin. "Okay. I get it. Yes, I might not have thought you were cheating exactly, but that's not far off from the truth of things. I was hurt and angry and irritated at you and despite all of that, I still couldn't understand why we weren't together."

"We were together, sweetheart," he said. Sarina felt his lips against her hair and sighed. "Even Lilith couldn't get in the way of what we have, not truly. She tried, I'll admit that. But in the end, I knew who my mate was, the woman I want for my wife."

"Will we ever get there?"

"Where?" he asked.

"Our wedding?"

"Let's try not to worry about it now. We'll trap that bitch in her own schemes, make sure our boys are good, and then, when the weather perks up and I can undress you with my eyes as you walk down the aisle, then we can get married."

"Alright," Sarina smiled, turning into him. They made love tenderly as the sun woke up in the east and then, after breakfast, the real planning began.

Chapter Six

Lilith smiled at the two little boys who slept in her bed. They were darling, like little pups who needed her tender loving care to grow up right. She almost couldn't imagine destroying them at the slightest annoyance, almost. "Sleep my little darlings," she sighed. "Because you're going to secure my prize for me, or die trying."

She sat in a chair near them and finally slept. Being up half the night with them before they'd finally settled down and slept had taken its toll on her. Still, she dreamed of the moment when Romeo had been informed that they were missing. It'd been far too easy to drug his daughter and her mate. The boys had been so fast asleep that they hadn't even woken up as they'd been plucked from their beds. It was like taking candy from a baby, and Lilith was disappointed there wasn't even as much as a small fight. Killing the great alpha's son had been an impulse… ripping out his daughter's throat would have been pure pleasure.

"Come to me," Lilith heard in her dreams. "Come to me Lilith. I know it's you I've always wanted. These last years I've had to settle for the best I could get, but now… now I know what I can have and that's you, darling."

"What about your pack?"

"My pack will do as I say. If I say you are my queen, they'll respect it and you. I'll pay Amanda handsomely for her time, but she'll not sit where you belong. Maybe we can keep her on as a concubine when we're feeling frisky for a threesome."

"Oh," Lilith smiled. "Now you're talking my language. I do enjoy a good love triangle, you know."

"Will you accept my rule?" Romeo asked.

"Certainly, darling. All I've ever wanted was to rule at your side. To be the queen I always knew I was. I impulsively went after Damon, knowing he'd be the first choice for alpha, but in my heart I always knew it was you I wanted. I'd lay awake at night, touching myself at the thought of being with you. Even after Damon and I were intimate, it never satiated my drive to mate with you."

"Excellent," he smiled. "Because lately I've grown weary of my wife and our family. There's a need inside me to return to the animal instincts. Mating should be more than just a casual, careful joining. There should be heat, passion, and a hell of a lot of rough sex involved."

Lilith couldn't have agreed more, as inside her dream she grew wet and ripe for him. She'd been dreaming of this night for as long as Romeo had been of age. He and Damon had been inseparable until she'd come along. Too late she'd realized it was Romeo she wanted and not his minutes older brother. Still, she couldn't deny that Damon had been a fun way to waste a few years. It'd taken Romeo that long to realize the darkness in her heart, slow by even a werewolf's standards. She'd hoped to turn him to her like her brother, but apparently he needed more time. It looked as if he was finally ready now though and she'd take full advantage of him while she was at it. She'd be more than queen. She'd be a freaking God to the Delta pack and in bed, she'd give Romeo the ultimate prize.

"Lilith!" Startled, Lilith shot up from the chair to the sound of the babies crying. Rubbing sleep from her eyes she remembered the two grandchildren she'd kidnapped from under the Delta pack's nose.

"I'm on it, Fenris," she groaned. Standing, she came to the boys and realized quickly that they definitely needed diaper changes. She'd never been the domestic sort and the thought of taking care of two little ones for longer than it took to reel in their grandfather was nearly overwhelming.

"I never realized how impulsive you are," he said, his dark eyes humored at her frustration. "Do you still plan on trying to snare him?"

"I'll have him one way or another, or no one will."

"You mean to tell me after twenty-four years, give or take some months that you're still so hung up on him that you can't see a life without him? What the hell has he done for you?"

"What have you done for me?"

"You infected me, you bitch," Fenris fumed.

He looked so damn sexy when he was angry, Lilith thought. Maybe she'd have them both. A woman's appetite needed tending after all.

"I gave you a gift," she said, her tone lethal. "I'll thank you not to forget it."

"How could I? I'm damned to change my shape, to be an animal, every damn time the moon becomes full. Did you ever stop to wonder at what you were doing?"

"Not really," she smiled. "That's the lovely part about being the queen that I am. I don't really have to concern myself with consequences. Hell, Fenris. Did it ever occur to you what we could have built if I hadn't died? I forgave you eons ago for your philandering. After all, it's the line that Romeo and Damon Traverse came from. But, we could have had a sweet little hierarchy if you'd kept your dick in your pants."

"Me? You were just as bad. You wouldn't meet with me when I wanted. What was I supposed to do?"

"Wouldn't meet you? It was you who couldn't keep me satisfied."

"Oh, I beg to differ," Fenris argued as she changed first Brody Jr. and then Jedidiah. She'd made bottles of goat's milk and handed one to Fenris. She took one of the twins and sat down to feed him. Fenris begrudgingly joined her. "I don't expect your memory to be flawless, especially after dying and all, but mine is still as sharp as a tack and I distinctly recall that you turned me away much more often than I ever did you. If fact, to my recollection, I never turned you away."

"You, Fenris, simply don't like to be second best and you're deathly afraid that if I take Romeo as my lover, you'll be forgotten in the wasteland of my past."

"Actually, I'm just waiting for you to realize that he can't give you what you want and I can."

"Oh, honey. If you could give me what I want, I wouldn't have to worm my way into Romeo's life, now would I?"

"Being an alpha's queen is as easy as mating with me."

"And can you give me the Delta pack? Easily the largest pack this side of the Delta River?"

"I can lay waste to their dreams and rebuild from the ashes a pack that's ten times as large and strong as the Delta pack only dreams of being."

"You talk a big, bad talk, Fenris, but so far I've only seen you lay waste to the outer rim of their pack. Show me something magical and perhaps you'll turn my attention back to you."

Fenris turned and taking the baby in his arms with him, walked away from her. He looked down at the squirming baby and grinned. "She has no idea what I can do to their pack, does she?"

He wouldn't hurt a baby like this, but Fenris knew that if he wanted the Delta pack to disperse, he'd have to make his next move serious. It would have to really hurt their heart and their numbers. He fed the little boy and then laid him down in his bed to sleep.

Fenris then left to meet with his pack to discuss the upcoming hunt. After their planning session, he dismissed them to gather their weapons and things and turned to check on the baby, noting Lilith's entrance as he did. "What the hell is going on? Your pack is the laziest excuse I've ever seen and yet everyone seems to be doing something today."

"We're going hunting," Fenris said simply. "Our stores are low and we obviously can't feed this horde without food."

"Werewolves hunt with the change."

"Yes," he smiled, as if he were talking to a slightly uncontrolled child. "But we both know our humans need food as well. Would you suggest I only feed my pack during the change?"

Her eyes, dark as her soul, were furious. "No. What do you plan to do with him?" Fenris looked at the boy sleeping on his bed.

"Put him with his brother. Don't twins need to be close when they're little? You wanted to kidnap them to make a statement and I'd say it worked well, but do you really want to scar them with Romeo coming your way? If you want him for your lover, the last thing you want to do is to harm his grandchildren."

He could tell she hated when his thoughts made sense. He could easily admit to letting her think him addle-brained, but the time for simply thinking was past. She wanted a man who could lead a pack and this was his time. He'd show her that Romeo Traverse had nothing on his cunning and tactical abilities, let alone his ability to lead and build a strong, worthy pack. The Delta wolves would join him or die; it was that simple.

Chapter Seven

Romeo stood at the edge of the woods looking into a clearing that by any human standards was beautiful and serene. The wolf in him knew much better. Out there lay a small pack that had nothing better to do with its time than plot how to kill off members of his own pack. And he was about to step out and ask their queen, for lack of a better word, to take him as her mate. And if that wasn't enough, he was going to stall her, protect his grandsons and do everything in his power to shove the entire pack to the depths of hell while he was at it.

He knew if he looked back, he wouldn't be able to see the members of his pack who waited in the woods, but he could feel them. He could hear Amanda whispering in his ear. He spoke back to her from his heart and then with a deep sigh, stepped into the clearing, holding his hands up as if in surrender.

"What do you want, Traverse?" Turning, Romeo saw a massive beta wolf standing guard over what looked like nothing more than a patch of meadow.

"I request an audience with Lilith Delaney," Romeo said. He kept his stance relaxed, even as his muscles bunched with tension.

"Tell me what you need her to know and I'll deliver the message."

"I'd think, considering I came all this way," he said, smiling, "that Lilith would appreciate seeing me in person. I'd hate to head home and find out later that she killed you for not telling her I was here."

Romeo watched the big man's eyes harden before he turned, tapped the grass twice with his foot and then squatted down. Romeo envisioned ripping the man's throat out while he was distracted, but that would be counterproductive to the pack's plan and it all hinged on him being the bait. "She'll see you in just a moment," the man said, standing up again. For his size and stature, he should have been an alpha, but Romeo knew Fenris well and Lilith, for that matter. Neither would subject themselves to adding more alphas to their pack than necessary. He could already see them fighting over the spot themselves.

"To what do I owe the extreme pleasure, Romeo?"

He turned to see Lilith, who'd obviously dressed for the occasion. Her body was outfitted with a dazzling silver dress that plunged low and tight over her considerable breasts, leaving nearly nothing to be desired. It curved out at her generous hips and had a slit up the thigh. Even from where Romeo stood, he could feel the sexual pull from her. Was that how she'd gotten Fenris, a much weaker man when it came to morals, to be seduced by her? He only knew of the legends, but asking her outright had its advantages.

"You have my grandsons for starters," he said, keeping his eyes from turning steely. His voice flowed out melodically, showing her he meant no harm. "And, I was hoping you might trade those two little ones for the bigger fish you want?"

"Oh?" she purred. She all but glided to him, her body now screaming with pheromones. Romeo, dampened down his own need, stomping it under his anger and frustration. "Well that's a thought now, isn't it? Although, I'd need to know, of course, why you're really here. It's certainly not just to trade yourself as a prisoner?"

"No," he said. Keeping his eyes on her, he smiled. "I've realized of late how tiring it can be to run a pack as large as the Delta. Seeing to everyone's needs is exhausting. Amanda can't get over the loss of our son and has left me rather dissatisfied, we'll say, in the bedroom. She's a darling woman and one hell of a witch, but I'm afraid we've come to an impasse in our relationship. Add the kids at home and the pack's needs and well, I've become quite dissatisfied by the whole lot of them."

"So you came here hoping to have a break?"

"Actually, I came, hoping that perhaps your pack might find room for an old alpha such as myself."

Her eyes went molten and Romeo felt the pull on his loins as if it was his first sexual encounter. It rivaled his first time with Amanda and that, he could readily admit, he hadn't been prepared for. Clamping a lid over his lust, Romeo sighed in relief when he felt Amanda reach out to him. *She's nothing but lies*, he heard her say in his head. Her love encased his heart, relieving some of the need Lilith pulled at in him.

"You'll forgive my skepticism of course," she grinned. "I've dealt with you before and well, I find myself in need of a little testing before I take you into my pack."

"Of course," Romeo said. Lilith stepped so close that he could smell the perfume she'd put on her body. Her dark eyes shimmered with hunger and a sexual need even he couldn't match. Not that he was particularly inclined to do so.

"Kiss me," she smiled. "Kiss me as if I'm the only woman in the entire Delta you want. If I believe you, I'll bring you in."

"And if you don't?"

"We'll deal with that after," she purred.

Romeo knew how to impress a woman, but this would be a test like none he'd ever had. Could he convince another woman, one who wasn't his mate, that he wanted her? Releasing some of the need she tugged at, Romeo tipped her face up at a slight angle, ignoring the darkness in her eyes, and took her mouth with a roughness he'd only ever shown Amanda. He felt her shock vibrate through him, but didn't respond to it, yet. His arm snaked around Lilith's waist and pulled her closer and he let his hand slide down to cup her tight ass. Sliding his tongue warmly over her full bottom lip, Romeo nearly groaned when she invited him deeper.

The kiss lasted far longer than he'd been prepared for and Romeo could feel both anger and hurt pumping through him when he pulled back, courtesy of his wife. "Well," Lilith smiled. "It's been a while since anyone's kissed me like that." He watched her run her tongue over her lip. "You certainly know what you're doing in that department. I suppose that's how you ended up with five kids. And I'm terribly sorry about your eldest by the way. I was fresh into my body and not quite in control of myself. I'd hoped to seduce him, but things went wrong rather quickly."

Romeo only nodded his head. Any forgiveness on his part, even for show, was too much. He'd already scarred his marriage by kissing her. He wouldn't doom it by forgiving her for Jason's death. "What will it be, Lilith?"

She smiled slowly, stepping closer and leaning into him. "I've waited decades for this. I'll take my time with you, but I'll release your grandsons in the meantime. I assume you have someone here who can take them?"

As planned, Amanda stepped forward from the woods. Her eyes showed the level of seething anger that poured through her and Romeo had to keep from grinning. One twitch of her eyebrow could have Lilith in a pile of ashes, but he knew his woman wouldn't give in to her own wants. "Oh," Lilith giggled outright. "I've always wanted to meet the former Mrs. Romeo Traverse. Tell me darling, is he as good in bed as I imagine? Don't worry about how things will go. He'll make sure you're taken care of. After twenty some odd years and five kids, I'd expect nothing less. And you'll find another mate soon enough. With a body like that, I'd offer a room next to mine so we could all have fun together, but I wouldn't expect you to accept. Playing second best to me would hardly be worthy of a former queen." Lilith then turned her attention to the massive guard. "Sarden! Bring the twins here."

"Yes, ma'am." The huge man Romeo had talked to moved quickly to an opening Romeo had noticed earlier but hadn't moved toward. Minutes later he emerged with two sleeping boys in his arms. Romeo stood still and let Amanda take them. She rushed forward, nuzzling them until they stirred. She cooed to them and Romeo flashed back to when Jason and Sarina had been born.

The Delta had been in the death grip of winter when Amanda had gone into labor. With a hospital too far away in the adverse conditions, Romeo had little choice but to find women to attend to her. Two older women, who had six babies between them, came to see about Amanda. She'd progressed quickly throughout the morning and by early afternoon things were happening at lightning speed.

"You push when you feel the urge, darling," one woman said to Amanda as she tucked another towel under Amanda's bottom. Three strong pushes had Sarina, with all her dark hair, emerging. She'd screamed like a banshee for a solid minute before she'd finally taken a breath and gained her color. Jason was right behind her and as soon as Sarina's cord had been cut, Amanda gave two pushes to have Jason entering the world. He'd been fair haired and nearly twice as large as his sister. Still, she outgunned him when it came to crying and once one got started they were both going, as if it was competition.

Chapter Eight

Romeo had never been more in love with Amanda than when she was birthing their children and the picture of her with their two grandsons in her arms nearly undid his resolve to see this through. What would it cost his marriage to be the bait to a woman who would certainly want him to bed her almost immediately?

Amanda turned to him, the twins tucked safely in her arms and Romeo knew the strength of their love in that moment, because her angry, frustrated eyes softened for just a moment. *Find a way to kill her*, Amanda said into his head. Then her hard shell was back and she turned from him to head back to the woods. As predetermined earlier, she walked a mile into the woods before Sarina had been allowed to come forward.

Romeo didn't know firsthand now, but he could imagine how joyful the reunion was between his daughter and soon to be son-in-law, and their twins. He'd give anything to have Jason back with him. Turning toward Lilith, Romeo knew it was now, or never.

"Shall we?" he asked.

She smiled and accepted his arm, leading him straight into the foyer of Hell.

Sarina didn't put Brody Jr. down or hand him to her mate without picking up or trading for Jedidiah. Even as her heart trembled for her father's safety, she couldn't contain the joy at having her sons back. "I didn't know that getting the twins back was part of the plan."

"It wasn't," Amanda said, her own eyes tortured by Romeo's absence. "Not originally anyways. But your father felt he had to try and it all worked out well. We'll have to trust that he can outsmart that bitch and do it before she catches on."

"What happened?" Sarina asked, picking up easily on her mother's discomfort.

"I sent my husband to be bait to a woman who wants to have him for herself. There's something particularly sick about all of this."

"He's doing it for all of us, Mama."

"Is that supposed to make it easier? To know that I'm sacrificing the man I love, the only man I've ever loved, so that our pack is safe and secure? I sacrifice my happiness for the sake of everyone? I know that sounds selfish, but that is how I feel right now."

"I'm not saying you should be all chipper about it," Sarina sighed. "I'm just saying that Daddy can handle himself. He knows what he's about with her."

"You didn't stand there and watch your mate kiss another woman as if she was the woman he truly wanted."

"He kissed her?"

"It was the way she tested him. She wanted to know for sure that he was telling the truth."

"Geez," Sarina sighed. "How'd that go?"

"He passed," Amanda said. "And I wanted to rip her head off. Even when he was reassuring me before and afterward, it didn't seem to help."

"I'm glad I had no idea she was inside Brody's head before she just appeared. I've wanted to claw her eyes out ever since for what she did to him and Jason."

"We all have a stake to claim when it comes to putting her down. I suppose when this is all said and done, we'll be able to claim it just as fiercely as the men. Although I'm grateful your father at least negotiated for the twins to be freed."

"Me too," Sarina said, gently touching the tops of her sleeping boys' heads. She followed her mother from her room and gently shut the door, checking once more to ensure the monitor was on. When the twins had gone missing, Brody had contracted two members of the pack to redo their windows, ensuring they were secured from the outside and inside as well. No one would slip into their home unannounced again. "How long does Daddy think it'll take to gain her trust?"

"He didn't say for sure, but I know he's counting the hours. The longer he stays with her, the sooner she'll know she's been snowed. I hope it's within the next forty-eight hours. Either way, I'll know when he knows."

"Well, you know you have the whole pack behind you. I've already sent couriers out to the outer most members to tell them. I wanted to give preference to those who've lost something or someone personal in this fight. If we can take out both Lilith and Fenris at the same time, it'll be over much sooner. I know that's a lot to ask though."

"Not when he murdered members of nearly twenty-five families. Those men know suffering that should have never touched them. Now at least they'll have their revenge. If it were up to me, I'd just let them have at it by overrunning that place. But I promised your father I'd do it this way first. He's got this one shot to undo that hellhound from her body so we can crush her. I've got this one chance to figure out how we crush her soul. So far, I've found nothing."

"The journals didn't say anything?"

"I've read through them all… from what I've read, there's nothing about destroying a soul, except from the person who is that soul. I'm not sure it can be done, not even by all four Radiants together."

"Well, we'll have to improvise then," Sarina smiled.

Sarina shared an impromptu lunch with her mother before she said farewell. Once the boys were safely home, she checked on them again and then, as night was falling, drew a hot bath. When she stepped out and was half dressed, Brody knocked on the door. "Come in."

"Wow," he said, looking her up and down.

"The boys still sleeping?" asked Sarina.

"I just fed and burped them. They're playing around the gated area downstairs. I came to make sure you hadn't fallen asleep."

"I'm fine," she chuckled. "Although indulging was nice for a change." She smiled when he stepped behind her and placed his chin on her shoulder.

"Does that work for both of us?" he asked before continuing. "The indulging part, that is…" Brody lifted his chin to press his warm lips against the nape of her neck. Chills ran over her skin at his touch.

"Not when our sons are awake," she laughed.

"Then kiss me to hold me over," he said, his voice already husky with unspent need. Giving in to her own want, Sarina leaned into him. Her mouth met his with enough passion to spontaneously ignite the Olympic torch. It flared hotly between them for a second, making them forget everything but their needs. Their bodies pressed together, fitting just the way they were intended... lips to lips, breasts to chest, hips to hip. Sarina moaned when she felt Brody's obvious erection and inwardly debated with herself even as she pulled back. Lightheaded, she gripped his arms tightly.

"You okay?"

"Fine," she said, grinning. "Just a little lightheaded. Can you check on the boys for me? I'll be down as soon as I'm dressed."

"Sure," he said, smiling.

After a quick kiss on her forehead, Sarina watched him head downstairs.

Chapter Nine

Romeo woke in his private quarters, thankful Lilith hadn't insisted he sleep with her in her chambers. He'd hidden the vials in a small space in the wall, next to the fireplace. Too emotionally worn out to worry about lighting a fire last night, his room felt damp and cold. Much of it still crude stone, it held the damp inside, making it easy to become chilled. Instinctively he built some kindling around the firewood and then lit up the flames that would eventually heat the room. Then, to save himself the trouble, he shifted into his wolf, almost instantly feeling the change within his body. While the wolf would eventually become chilled after too long in the damp, Romeo knew in the long run, the wolf would have survived where the human would falter.

"Cold much?" he heard a soft female voice then some laughing come from the doorway. He turned toward Lilith and whined in response. Today she was decked out in tight, ass hugging jeans and a tank top that, when coupled with her sexual pull, made it impossible for him not to notice her large breasts. Biting his tongue, Romeo thought of Amanda and instantly felt her connect to him.

Hang in there babe. You can do this. You're an alpha, my alpha. Don't let that bitch spoon feed you lies. She's all lies, remember nothing but them. I love you.

Sighing, Romeo looked up into eyes as dark as the abyss. Feeling overwarm, he grabbed a blanket in his teeth and changed back to his human self, using the large blanket to cover himself. When Lilith smiled and stepped further into his room, he groaned. "I forgot to light a fire last night so it was damp when I woke up."

"I see," she purred. "Feeling much warmer now though. Tell me, Romeo, has it been that long since a woman's bedded you right?"

He didn't need to look down to know that he'd grown hard. What she didn't know was that it was Amanda's voice in his head that had turned him on and nothing to do with her. She was full of lies, just as his mate had said. Still, he had a part to play if they wanted to end this before it truly began. Fenris was already up one on them for the women and children he'd murdered the weeks before.

"Amanda and I find ourselves stifled somewhat by our older children. Now with the young twins over so much, our ability to express ourselves is less than desirable."

"Well," she said, stepping closer to him. Her hand tugged at the blanket until Romeo let it fall. "There are things I can do to help you remember what it can be like."

"I appreciate that Lilith," he stumbled. Before he could elaborate, her lips fused to his, her hand snaking down to cup him. Her hand stroked him so easily, that Romeo had to bite himself to pull away from her. "I'm sorry. I… I'm not sure I'm quite ready for all of that."

"It's alright," she said, obviously irritated. "There's time. At least I know that you can still perform, and rather nicely if my hands have anything to say about it. Even Damon wasn't that well-endowed." Lilith said, making herself comfortable on his bed. It was pointless to ask her to leave. Right now, for all intents and purposes, she was the alpha.

"Is there something, other than sex, that I can do for you Lilith?"

"Actually," she smiled. "I was hoping we could hunt today. I know we can't go near your pack, but the vampire in me is dangerously hungry and I'd hate to drain one of my own."

Romeo just stared at her, shocked. He didn't know much about vampires but that revealed a lot about his nemesis. "How… how did you start a line of werewolves if you're a vampire?"

"That story is going to require a lot of wine," she giggled. "And a wager."

"A wager?"

"Always," she said, a glint of hunger in her eyes. "I'll make do with pig's blood tonight while I capture your imagination. Then, come morning, if I'm still telling you my story, you have to mate with me. Make me your official queen."

Romeo needed this information, desperately. But could he risk so much? He needed counsel and fast.

"Why don't you go get the wine chilling and I'll take some time to consider your wager. What do I get if you're not still talking come morning?"

"I'll give you the best head you've ever had," Lilith said, running her tongue over her lips seductively, before she turned and headed out.

Sitting down, Romeo tried to enter a state of silent meditation. His mind whirled with possibilities so that he had to clamp down on his control to get even close to meditating. Eventually though, he was able to reach out to Amanda.

Amanda, can you hear me, sweetheart? Her answer came sleepily. *She's duped me into wagering sex with her. If she wins she wants me to make her my mate. If I win, she's promised to give me head, which obviously the potion will work for. I'm just not sure this wager is one I should take.* Amanda asked about the wager.

She's going to tell me how she came to infect Fenris and start the line that became ours. Romeo was met with silence for more than a minute before Amanda answered him.

~Do it.

~You're sure?

~We can't afford to forego that information. Do whatever you have to Romeo. Use the potions I gave you wisely. The odor will last an entire day, but too

often and she'll be onto you. We're working our end as much as possible, but we need to know her beginnings.

A few minutes later Lilith returned with a large wine bottle in an ice bucket and two wine glasses. She was dressed in a creamy camisole that left her shapely legs bare and hugged her incredible body. If it hadn't been against his better judgement, Romeo would have backed into a corner, as far away from her as possible.

"Shall we?" she asked. Romeo took the wine she offered and after sniffing it, took a considerable gulp. It didn't go down like whiskey, but the alcohol burned warmly enough in his gut.

"Please," he said, helping her sit.

Chapter Ten

Amanda paced up and down the length of the room she shared with Romeo. It was just about the only place she found comfort nowadays. She was increasingly thankful that both Briana and Lucia were able to come and offer their aid. She still felt as if they were grasping at straws when it came to making solid plans to disrupt Lilith's soul from her body. Destroying her flesh would be easy. It was the destruction of her soul Amanda knew they had to get right if they wanted to rid themselves of her forever. And that didn't even include doing the same to Fenris. If they could get those two permanently taken care of, it'd be easy to rule over what was left of their pack.

Hopefully they'd make a nice addition to the Delta pack, helping to fill occupations that had been left empty when Fenris made his first attack. "Mama?" Sarina said, knocking on the door.

"Come in," she answered.

"Everything okay?"

"I'm just trying to think. Nothing I've read or known previously speaks about the destruction of the soul. It's always something the owner must do.

Although I would think Lilith had already passed that point by now."

"So, if her soul was to be destroyed, how did she make her way back from the depths of hell?"

Sarina looked at her mother, who was now smiling broadly. "Oh darling, you're a genius! She is Lilith, but she's not the same, not nearly."

"Okay," Sarina said, not convinced that she helped at all.

"When someone dies we usually expect one of two exits. One of light and the other darkness. Lilith obviously went to the darker side. However, I don't think she went exactly the way we think. What if she didn't make the entire fall, but landed somewhere in between? What if she got stuck somewhere that allowed her to *climb* her way back out?"

"How'd she climb out with a body then?"

"I believe, because she obviously wasn't destroyed completely, that the body she had, the one we buried, was brought back to her. If she never truly went to hell, she wasn't ever truly dead to begin with."

"So she pops out of Brody's mind into her same body that was buried twenty some odd years ago?"

"Yes," Amanda squealed. "Which means she's not nearly as strong as she'd like to believe. Her body is extremely weak and I'm sure it's some sort of magic that has her looking as good as she does. We've all aged some, but being in a coma-like state for more than two decades had to take its toll on her body. I need some quiet time so I can reach your dad. He needs to know this. Go get Brody and everyone else together. Our first stage is complete. We need to get your dad out of there, now."

Sarina headed upstairs, snagging Brody on the way to the living room. "What's up?" he asked when he saw her coming.

"Mom's figured out some things and says our first stage is complete. She's obviously worried about Dad being discovered or worse. Eventually Lilith will realize that he's toying with her, avoiding her, and she'll come unglued. While that could play to our advantage, it could put Dad in jeopardy and I'm sure Mom wants to avoid that altogether."

"I don't doubt it," he agreed. "Need me to make any calls?"

"Yes," she smiled. "Can you call all my aunts and uncles? Also, see if you can get my siblings around as well. I'm going to contact the other Radiants, save Aunt Pen."

"I'm on it," he said, pressing a quick kiss to her lips. She felt the want of him in that fleeting moment. Lately with everything going on it'd been too crazy to do much about being together intimately. The last time had been more of an emotional need than physical, but with the twins back and things moving forward with Lilith now, Sarina found that her lips tingled whenever Brody kissed her and that her system, one that had felt asleep for too long, was waking up and turning on.

Sarina made her calls, explaining to both her Aunt Lucia and Aunt Briana what was going on. They promised to offer their aid in bringing an evil such as Lilith to her doom. "Your mother became a surrogate mother for us when we lost our mothers," Briana said.

"That's right," Lucia agreed, enjoying the three-way call. "She took care of us, taught us how to use our powers, became our leader and so much more."

"Thank you both," Sarina said before hanging up. She came out of the family room to find Brody standing there, his dark eyes soaking her in.

"Everything okay?" asked Sarina.

"Walk with me?" countered Brody.

"Alright," she agreed. "How are the boys?"

"Shawna's watching them. Last I saw, they were both sleeping peacefully."

"I owe that bitch if nothing more than for the torture she put us through. Safe and sound or not, my boys were taken from me."

"We'll make her pay," Brody offered, taking her hand in his. "You can be sure of that."

"I plan to be," Sarina added.

"Can we take a break from war tonight?"

"Sorry," she added. "I guess I'm just a little revved. Knowing now what we do, I'm anxious to get started.

The sooner we get my dad out of there and see to her demise, the better off we'll be."

"I agree," Brody added. "I also think that my wife and I need some time together."

Sarina giggled when his hand slid up her side to cup her breast. "We just spent time together."

"And I'm thinking it's been too long already," he laughed. "We haven't been intimate nearly enough lately. Don't you miss that passion?"

"Of course I do," she smiled, turning into his embrace. "But that doesn't mean I've forgotten my boys or the extension of my family. It's not easy to concentrate on being together when I just got my boys back and my father is almost a prisoner to a devil woman."

"I know," he sighed. "That's why we need this time. I don't want our relationship to fall victim to this bitch along with everything else."

"And you think not being intimate will do just that?"

"Do you remember our last time?"

"Not clearly," she said, understanding his point.

"When was the last time we really made love? I'm not talking about filling a need, or expressing an emotional issue. I'm talking about really sinking into one another so that the whole world falls away and it's just the two of us?"

"Probably not since Lilith kidnapped your mind."

"Exactly," Brody said, rubbing his thumbs over her hands. "Don't you think we need something just between the two of us that makes us strive for more than just a mediocre marriage?"

"Lots of people have great marriages when the passion of sex has waned"

"Name one," Brody challenged her. When she couldn't, a giggle rose in her throat.

"Okay, okay." Surrendering, she added, "I get where you're coming from, I do. I'm just not sure I'm ready yet and I don't want to disappoint you by just showing up physically."

Sarina could tell Brody was frustrated. His whole body tensed as he took in what she was saying. "Alright," he sighed, clearly let down. When he turned away, Sarina struggled with whether to let him go.

"Brody," she called. When he turned around, she went to him. "I love you and I want our marriage to be incredible. I know that we need time and I know that we've both been extremely stressed out. Right now I just can't make that go away. If I could just flip a switch and make it all better, I would. I'd jump you in a hot minute, but I can't. I can't forget that we just got the twins back, safe and sound, thank God. But my dad is still out there, trying to keep that woman content without destroying himself and his own marriage. I need to be able to put all that away before I can give all of myself to you, to this."

Sarina sighed when she saw his pretty blue eyes soften. His hand came up to cup her cheek. "I get it," he said, pressing a warm kiss to her lips. They walked back into the house just as Sarina's siblings were coming downstairs.

Chapter Eleven

Romeo knew he was in deep crap when Lilith pulled out the third bottle of wine. Six hours into her tirade about life as a wicked mix of vampire and werewolf and she had yet to pause for more than a moment. He couldn't use the vials and this crazy bitch showed almost no signs of being even slightly inebriated.

"So," Lilith smiled as she filled their glasses again. "There I was, just eighteen and I knew that this place was special. I knew I wanted to settle here, but I had no idea what was in store for me, even when Fenris came along. I stepped into a bar one night and there he was, smoking hot and arrogant enough to get my attention. He smelled amazing and I could hear the blood pumping through his veins. It was my first major test, going into public with this voracious need to feed inside of me.

"He asked me to dance and I accepted. We were inseparable all night and I was more than happy to accept his invitation to go back to his place. Being a vampire doesn't satiate that need for sexual excitement, of course, so I was all too ready when his actions asked for more than just a goodnight kiss. I think I nearly killed him that first night. We played house for a solid week, screwing on every surface in his house and some outside before I showed him what I truly was."

Romeo could just imagine how that turned out. "He ran didn't he?"

"Like a little bitch," she laughed, sipping her wine. "He even screamed like one when I caught him by the collar of his shirt. I leapt on him, pinning him to the forest floor, but I knew, even before I bit him, that I wouldn't drain him. I wanted to share the gift I had inside of me. Even scared like he was, I could feel his erection. I pulled up my dress and slid over him, riding him until he came. Then I bit him and as the poison filled his blood I made him bite me back. That's when we became mates."

"So that's where the mating ritual came from. Mates have to bite each other to make a mark, like marking a territory."

"I guess you could look at it that way, yes," Lilith said. "After he'd bitten me I let go, jerked him up and nearly dragged him back to the house. He fought the poison, which is never a good idea, but I couldn't make him understand that. It took nearly three days for him to start looking and acting normal and after that he seemed somehow okay with what I was." Lilith paused for a moment to recollect her memories.

"He said he felt incredible, but neither of us knew yet what would happen really. When the full moon came up a week later, Fenris went through his first change and it was amazing to watch. I knew in that moment that I wanted an army of werewolves and now

I knew how to get them. That night, while he hunted, so did I. I found a gorgeous woman who was slightly less intelligent than average. She was innocent in so many ways and especially sexually. I befriended her rather easily and after a few glasses of wine, I asked if she'd like to come back to my place. She accepted and on the way home I asked if she'd ever been intimate with a woman.

"She giggled and shook her head. I kissed her then and slid my hand up her thigh. It didn't take long to have her so aroused that she couldn't see straight. I brought her into Fenris' home and seduced her even further. The first time she came, I let her enjoy it. Then I taught her how to pleasure me in return. Surprisingly she was a quick learner and we enjoyed each other immensely. The next morning before Fenris made it back, I took her again. This time I bit her and when she bit me in return, I came hard knowing I'd have my first line of wolves."

"What happened after that?" Romeo asked, encouraging her to continue. Close to dawn or not, he needed to know everything she'd tell him. He poured them each another glass of wine and her sharp eyes smiled at him, holding a sense of evil even he couldn't grasp.

"Fenris came back home and knew I'd been up to something. He opened the door to my room and groaned. When I explained what I wanted and that I'd brought her home to be his mate, I could tell he was horny. She was obviously in no condition at that point to oblige him, so I did. By the time she healed, Fenris, unbeknownst to me, had already impregnated me." Lilith took the glass of wine that Romeo filled and gulped down half the glass.

"Still, being ravenous for a line of wolves to do my bidding, I offered her to him and they mated. She turned on the following full moon and I became a little jealous you could say. Every full moon for the next year I found and turned as many people as I could, joining us all together. I excavated a network of caves that would hold us all rather comfortably, until my new wolves could control themselves. By then I'd delivered my first hybrid. Fenris' mate had had a set of twins and several of our other wolves were expecting or close to delivering. Soon after that, Fenris' mate was killed on a hunt and after we mourned her passing, I took him as my mate."

"Wow," Romeo said, truly blown away by the beginnings. "That's quite a legacy."

"I'm not through yet," she said. "There is still some time before morning, although I can feel the sun beginning to rise." Lilith took a moment to stretch her arms and legs, oozing sexuality. Romeo took a sip from his wine glass to avoid staring. He thought of Amanda to ward off Lilith's efforts.

"What I didn't know during those first years, was that Fenris had an appetite that was nearly insatiable. We screwed all the time, producing several wolf pups for our pack. Fenris, however, had a whole new pack under his rule as well… one I had no idea about. Your line came from that pack and although the branches from it fizzled out some over the years, your lineage has remained strong, stronger than most of the packs east of the Delta."

"Is that why you've been obsessed with me? Because you knew Damon wouldn't rule?" Romeo said, coming to understand fully how devious and evil Lilith really was. "You encouraged him in the black arts, didn't you? You knew if he got too far down, he'd destroy himself and I'd take over as alpha."

"It didn't take much, really," Lilith said, her eyes honest and sober.

Romeo felt his stomach turn and his chest tighten.

"After you tried to kill me, I let him believe it for a time. It fueled his anger, made the perfect platform for me to introduce black magic. I did it subtly, without him knowing it was me. I knew the first thing he'd try was to bring me back, so after a few weeks of practicing, I let him believe that it had finally worked. After that, he couldn't get enough and actually became very good as a magician. Had he not been so soft I might have used him much more often, for more than just good sex." Lilith flashed a wicked smile, one that made Romeo hate her for how she treated his brother.

"Still, I knew after a time that his heart was too dark to be what I needed in a mate. I let him continue on in his revenge, knowing it'd eventually doom him to destruction. When your father passed the alpha position to you, I knew instantly that I wanted to have you as my mate. Before I could introduce myself as someone else entirely, someone you'd approve of, you went and found that little wench. I was flabbergasted by how quickly you'd talked her into mating with you and knew you must be something incredible in bed for a girl like her to completely unravel her whole world for you. Still I couldn't just usurp all your plans. I'm a hybrid vampire wolf, but there are still some things even I can't do."

"So you've waited all this time to be with me?" asked Romeo.

"I knew eventually she wouldn't be enough for you. I knew you'd need much more than she could give you, witch or not. She's still much more human than either of us and you need a woman who truly understands you," Lilith said, sliding onto her knees. "It looks, Romeo, as if you win. The sun is coming, but my story is over and it isn't yet dawn."

Romeo watched Lilith unsnap his jeans with a single twist of her wrist. Fighting the part of him that was drawn to her, he bit the inside of his cheek hard, until he tasted the metallic flavor of his blood. Coughing hard, he spit the blood into his hand. "Lilith," he said, coughing again. "I'm not at my best for fellatio or any other niceties right now."

Her dark eyes glinted like steel as a smile spread over her face. Grabbing his hand in a vice-like grip, she flexed his palm and ran her tongue over it, lapping up the blood like a pup to water. "Mm," she moaned. "You're so rich." Her hands pinned him to the bed and her mouth fused to his as she slid her body over his.

"Lilith," Romeo begged. "I can't…"

"Oh, you can, Romeo. Don't you feel what's inside you? It's begging to be free to run wild as only I can let it. Be with me. Be with me this one time and I promise you'll never look back."

Her mouth closed around him before he could regain his ability to move and Romeo knew if he didn't get out now, he never would. "Lilith," he breathed. She giggled as his cock slid into her mouth so deep that he could feel the back of her throat pulsing against him. Grabbing the wooden stick he'd set under his pillow, Romeo called her again. "Lilith baby."

He coaxed her off his dick and smiled, leaning forward. He ran his tongue playfully along her collarbone and over her neck and jaw. Then he kissed her until he felt her body relax. Pulling back, he used all of his strength to hit her across the face with the flat of the stick. He heard her howl in pain as he ran through the caves. Over the last week, he'd mapped them out rather well in his head, but he'd never been allowed near the exits. With that she-devil on his tail, he knew if he didn't find an exit soon, she'd kill him quickly and painfully.

Making the change on the run brought a whole new level of agony as he felt his bones crack and shift. He rounded a bend in the cave and saw light streaming in from the exit ahead. Leaping, he caught one guard with his claws as his teeth ripped the other one apart. Romeo burst into a clearing and just kept running, knowing that the she-devil and her hell hounds would be after him.

<<<>>>

Amanda woke with a start just as dawn crept over the ridge. She knew instantly that it was Romeo and before she could reach out to him, she heard him in her head.

~I'm coming, darling. But we need the first line of defense.

~I'm on it. Just keep heading home...

Amanda scrambled to dress and was calling everyone as she ran downstairs. "Romeo's on his way, but Lilith is hot on his heels with Fenris' pack. We need everyone we've got. Shawna, you stay with the twins."

Wolves poured out of the house as others came from all four sides of the Delta region, swarming in like ants to defend their alpha's home and life. Tense and ready, several wolves made the change, howling through the pain as the Radiants worked their magic. Briana brought a hurricane ripping through the forest so that trees lost their leaves and branches snapped. At Sarina's request, Penelope put up a wind barrier over a small cottage and its land that was centered in the woods. Not only would it be safe from the other Radiants' magic, but the onslaught of Lilith's wolves would move around it as well. She didn't elaborate, but Penelope wondered correctly if Sarina was protecting Brandt, a man who'd once disguised himself as Brody to try and impregnate her. She heard bits of the story and knew that Sarina and Brandt had made peace with each other, a feat she was sure she wouldn't have done as easily.

"He's coming!" Amanda shouted as she stretched out her hands. The earth began to tremble just as Romeo broke through the trees. He was sprinting, his dark coat glistening with sweat and shining green eyes focused on the line of wolves that would meet him.

Come on babe, Romeo heard in his head. Fueled by his pack, Romeo picked up his sprint and leaped over the first line of defense just as Amanda pulled up a massive line of earth. He watched as Amanda lifted the earth high into the air and then dropped her hands forcefully, bringing the line of earth back to itself like shaking out a tablecloth. Lilith's wolves tried everything to stop before the fall into the abyss Amanda had opened up. The ones who'd found themselves in the air lay broken and bruised, if not dead, on the ground.

Lucia sent flames of fire-like lightning from the sky and instantly consumed any wolf who couldn't move fast enough to evade her. Still, Romeo knew that Lilith and Fenris were far back, keeping themselves clear of the mayhem. They'd live to fight another day as Romeo sent his wolves out to pick off the weaker ones who'd be easy prey. The skirmish lasted another hour as the Radiants made sure that every last wolf that had been left was taken care of. Lucia stayed the longest, incinerating the remaining wolves who had been left only half changed, dying in pain as their bodies fluttered in the change. When she finally came inside, Romeo wasn't the only one who noticed the toll it took on her.

"It's never easy using our powers to give someone the respite of death," Amanda said, wrapping an arm around Lucia, who quickly turned into her shoulder and cried. Romeo watched with both admiration and love as his wife comforted the young woman. Barely a woman at all when her mother had been killed, Lucia had found in Amanda the mother figure she'd needed to enter adulthood with both grace and dignity. Briana too, had looked to Amanda for much guidance as she stepped into the powers her own mother had passed to her. It was something Romeo rarely commented on, but knowing what he'd stood to lose, he knew he needed to take the time to tell his wife just how amazing she was.

Chapter Twelve

Sarina didn't argue when her father asked that she and Brody keep the twins in the house and stay over for a while. She knew he worried about Lilith and Fenris attacking again in their anger. He'd bought and erected massive tents to house the entire Delta pack on the land his father had owned before they'd expanded; the Radiants had also worked together to make a force field around the encampment. As long as one of them was awake, the protection surrounding them would hold, so they took turns sleeping.

"You look tired," Amanda said as Sarina came into the kitchen.

"I'm exhausted, but more so emotionally than physically," she sighed. Opening the fridge, she pulled out a piece of double chocolate fudge cake she'd saved from dinner.

"Wanna talk about it?"

Sarina smiled. She'd always been able to tell her mother anything without fear of being judged for it. "Brody wants to be intimate and I'm afraid, terribly afraid, that I can't give him what he needs." Sarina waited for her mother to interrupt and when she didn't, Sarina continued. "When the boys went missing, something changed inside of me. I'm not the woman I was before they were kidnapped. Even inside of myself I feel hard, as if all the soft places turned to stone so that I'd be able to deal with the aftermath if that bitch had hurt them. Now I can't seem to soften any of those places again, not even for Brody."

"You two need time together," Amanda said, her green eyes so like Sarina's. "Take this and find your mate. I promise it'll help you find your center."

Sarina looked at the key in her mother's hand. "What is it?"

"It unlocks a door that no one, until now, has known about. Both you and Brody need to find what you lost when your sons were kidnapped. I made this special place when Jason was killed because I was losing myself as well. Your father will use it soon too, but tonight, you and Brody need it. And don't worry about the boys. Shawna is watching them and our whole pack is here. Take tonight, Sarina, so that you'll have a tomorrow to look forward to."

Sarina did as her mother said and found Brody sitting in the family room, sipping scotch. Grabbing his hand, she put his scotch down and pulled him up with her. She turned and tucking his hand in hers, let the key lead her where they needed to go. "What's up?" he asked, curiosity in his voice.

"We're going to find ourselves," was all Sarina said as the key warmed in her hand. Finding a beautifully carved door in a recessed wall of the basement, Sarina stuck the key in. The door opened without further provocation and both Sarina and Brody stepped into a radiant and breathtaking light.

"Welcome," came a voice Sarina recognized. She looked up to see the woman from her dreams in what seemed like ages ago. She'd been in the grips of terrible evil when this beautifully stunning woman had given her three realities to choose from. After every visit, which lasted twenty-four hours only, Sarina had been forced to choose the reality she wanted most. Thankfully she'd followed her heart and things had settled back down for her, until recently. "Your mother summoned me in her need to help her find herself again. It's common for gifted people and those in a vulnerable point in their lives to need a center to tie them to this realm. When that center is lost or somehow disrupted or forgotten; things can change and rarely for the better. Take my hands and remember your center."

Sarina reached out and took the woman's hand, encouraging Brody to do the same. Light washed through the room and Sarina noticed that they were both wearing bright white robes. "See and remember," echoed the woman's voice. Sarina and Brody walked hand in hand over a hill and saw themselves below. They were locked in each other, their first time making love. It washed through them, the love of that first time, the way they'd touched and held each other. Sarina felt tears stream down her face when the picture changed and she'd been arguing with her father about mating with Brody. Then came the day she'd found out about the twins and telling Brody. The pregnancy memories came next, how they'd loved each other fiercely as their sons grew strong and healthy in her womb.

By the time their memories slowed down, both Sarina and Brody had found the love that flowed between them. The stunning white fizzled away and they turned to see a gorgeous room decked out in deep reds that shimmered like water. Sarina was so thankful for a mate that knew her so well. She followed Brody into the room and locked out everything but this moment with him. Her mother had once again been so right. They'd needed this and neither of them would turn away the answer to finding their center again.

Brody knew he'd never seen Sarina like this, vulnerable. She was an alpha's daughter and had always been the stronger of them. Pulling her close, Brody kissed her cheeks, forehead, eyebrow ridges, and jawline. His hands barely touched her as he took them both slowly into that first shower of arousal. He grinned when her arms came almost lazily around him. He swallowed her sigh when his mouth came to hers. It wasn't the soul scorching passion he thought he'd missed. Instead, it drenched him, searing him with a tenderness he'd never experienced before, not even with her.

Neither of them needed words and Brody used his mouth to entice her, running his warm tongue over her lips. She opened to him, taking him into her with a trust he'd never had to ask for. That was the wonderful thing about their love. It gave willingly, without expecting anything in return.

Smiling, Brody knew they needed the night and eased back when Sarina started to rush. He had her lay on the floor that felt amazingly like a bed, even though it didn't look like one. It was warm and welcoming, much like his mate. He noticed too, how the room changed with their mood. The smell of jasmine permeated the air, saturating his senses as blue and green hues flowed around Sarina. Brody worked to arouse her, using everything he had at his disposal to do so. The love, that deep red they'd seen was still there, but now it was at the edges, settling in to await its expression. The more he ripened Sarina, the more she ebbed out deep blues and brilliant greens. When his hand cupped her breast, Sarina bowed up against his touch and those bold colors splashed over the walls as she moaned.

Aching for her, Brody didn't stop her when she sat up to touch him. His own arousal expressed itself in bright oranges and shimmering reds and yellows. She stripped his clothes, needing to feel his flesh as much as he wanted her to. Her warm lips traveled over his skin and Brody found for the first time, the trembling anticipation he'd never known before her. Her mouth found him almost impossibly hard and her lips and tongue slid over his tip. Her low moans of approval only fueled the chains that yanked at his control. He nearly begged her to stop as she took him deeper. Her warm lips slid over him, moving up and down in a way that made Brody's vision blur.

His own moans ripped through him as his mate continued to go down on him. His hands sank into her dark, silky hair, massaging her head and tugging at those beautiful, wavy curls as she slowly tortured him. His breathing hitched as she pushed him too close to the edge. Yanking back, Brody heard her yelp in pain. "Sorry, I'm sorry, Sarina," he pleaded. "I can't…" Already too close, Brody was left breathless when he tumbled over that steep ledge and spent himself.

Looking up, Brody saw Sarina's eyes glowing in the light. Gone were the blue and green colors of her arousal. Now there was nothing but deep, almost blood red all around her. It took Brody no time at all to realize that this was the color of her hurt, the color of her doubt and fear. Rising to his knees, he approached her slowly. He didn't speak, but let his caress, his gentle touch speak for him.

His hand came under her chin, raising it so she'd look at him. Then he kissed her, slowly coaxing her response. Flicking his tongue back and forth over her full mouth, Brody sighed when she opened to him. He sank into her now, fueled by a new need to fulfill her, to satisfy her in a way he'd never known she needed until now. He kissed her until her hands sought his flesh, then, laying her back, Brody touched her everywhere. He ignited her passion so that she was writhing, even before he sought her hot, bubbling center with his fingers. He filled her, finding her clit and enjoying the way she moaned when he touched her there. Within minutes, Brody's rhythm had her climaxing.

Still, he found her insatiable and his own need overwhelmed him. His cock throbbed and he knew an entirely new level of need when his tip found her wet pussy and he took her with one deep, hard thrust. She reared up against him as blue and green washed through the room, sweeping over the walls and nearly blinding him. His hands gripped her lovely hips as he plunged into her over and over again. She met him now, her own need demanding its own satisfaction.

"Brody!" Sarina cried, her body trembling on the brink of shattering. He used his skill now to show her all he knew about her, all he'd learned in their short but tumultuous time together.

"Come with me, Sarina," he begged, his own body teetering on that shaking precipice. Thrusting into her, relentless in his pursuit of her, Brody felt her body tighten around him as she came, her orgasm ripping through him like a tornado. He met her in that moment, spending himself deep inside her, sharing in something greater than themselves. Looking down at her, this woman who meant the world to him, he noticed the way the color around them was a warm purple, flowing around them like water.

After a few moments, Brody lifted her in his arms, carrying her to an open door that led to a spacious hot spring. Like a secluded lagoon, steam rose to the surface of the bluest water he'd ever seen. Bird song filled the air with sweet, relaxing melodies and Brody inhaled heavily the scent of lavender and chamomile. "Your mother really knows how to do up a room," he chuckled.

"I don't think she did this. I think this room provides whatever the person using it needs."

"Like virtual reality?"

"Something like that, yes."

"Can we stay here forever?"

"No," Sarina laughed, circling his neck with her arms. "I don't mind staying until morning though." Drawn into her, Brody stepped into the spring with Sarina still cradled in his arms. They made the most of the room and their time together, rediscovering each other with a newness they cherished. When dawn came and they stepped back into real time, Brody and Sarina did so, knowing each other in a way they never would have without this experience.

Chapter Thirteen

Lilith sat seething next to Fenris, who looked rather happy just to have survived. If vampires could spontaneously combust, she certainly would have, such was the level of her anger. "What the hell was that?"

"It was a well-planned defense," Fenris replied. None but a few of their pack had survived and now there was no war to mount as they had no soldiers. "You can't blame them, you know."

"Shut up, Fenris. Romeo Traverse played me for a fool and I will have my revenge on him."

"Please," he scoffed. "You have no chance of besting the Delta pack, especially now. All of our warriors were killed in one fell swoop. How exactly do you plan to destroy them now?"

Lilith knew only one way to have the army she needed and it'd cost her everything she was to get it. "What do you know of the black magic, Fenris?"

"Only that it will strip you of your very soul, given enough time."

"True," she smiled. "But it's worth it to see those two and their entire pack grovel at our feet."

Lilith knew Fenris probably didn't agree, but she didn't care. She was the queen and that little trollop Romeo ran with would pay for her insolence. And there was nothing more vicious than a woman who'd been scorned. Romeo had no idea who he was toying with. He would soon enough though, of that she was certain.

Finding the ancient texts that included the black magic, Lilith spent hours poring through them, studying them. She'd be ready the next time she faced Romeo and he'd have a hell of a time stopping her then. Lilith knew she'd been angry and foolish this last time, of that she could readily admit. But this next time, she'd wait until the perfect moment and she'd strike when he least expected it.

She already knew she wanted Amanda Traverse to suffer at Lilith's own hands. That conniving bitch had it coming to her for the lives she took today. Lilith didn't care how long it took her, as she'd have all the time in the world, until it was done. She knew firsthand what hell looked like and she'd not only seen it, but survived. Selling her soul shouldn't be too difficult, as the man in charge seemed to prefer it that way. No fuss when someone died, she guessed. That night Lilith dreamed for the first time since coming back to herself.

The woods where she walked were dark as fog rolled over like waves in the ocean. Thick and heavy, Lilith found it increasingly hard to breathe. She called out, but no one came, not that she'd truly expected anyone to. The earth beneath her feet began to soften, holding her feet like vices. She sank down into the muck, screaming as it pulled her down past her chest and neck. When her face became covered, she knew instantly that she was dying, would die this time with no chance of having her revenge.

The lower she went, the more screaming she heard. It wasn't the excited screams of love and joy, but rather the terrified, horrid screams of pain and fear. They clawed at her own resolve as heat permeated her bones but didn't kill her. Her joints shrieked as she fell deeper and deeper into this pit of darkness with only the continuous screeching of others to keep her company.

Finally, a light illuminated the area where she was and Lilith came face to face with the reality of hell. Countless souls of people who'd once lived mostly decent lives mourned their very existence in perpetual terror. Their pain, every level of it, was almost permanently etched on their faces. Everywhere she turned, they begged her to take them back with her, anything to escape this eternity. The stench of death saturated her senses so that breathing made her want to vomit.

"Lilith," she heard as she continued to sink down. "Why, Lilith?"

"Who are you?"

"Oh, come now. You know who I am. Everyone knows who I am. I'm the things nightmares are made of," came the singsong voice that stretched her nerves. Light was everywhere, a misty, hazy light that made her skin crawl. "Why now, when I gave you exactly what you asked for?"

She knew instantly who she was talking to now. The Devil had come to collect his debt and she'd have to pay it. She loathed the very idea, but she had sold her soul. One could hardly escape from that, now could they? "You're a liar. I didn't get what I wanted. I only got the illusion of it."

His laughter bubbled out, making her body scream in pain, its edge sharpened to the point of killing without death. "Deceit is my best and favorite attribute, you know. I'm so glad you noticed. Do you think I amassed this kingdom by being righteous? No, darling. I've roamed the Earth for thousands of years, plucking and picking those I wanted. Thankfully as generations passed and time moved quickly onward, the plucking and picking became more like harvesting. Instead of a few souls to take, I found humanity sinking further and further into depravity, making my job all the easier. Now I simply sit back and wait for your puny, insignificant lives to snuff out and down you fall."

"Not everyone," Lilith said, almost as a defense.

"Oh no," he sighed. "There are still those who are and will probably forever be unreachable. Pure souls that seek the light and forsake the darkness. However, given how things have turned out for me, I don't mind them so much. The darkness has overcome the light in your world now and I bathe in the wickedness of the times, such as they are. The more evil prevails up there, the more residents I get down here, so you can see now why I'm an extremely tolerant host."

"What do you want from me?"

"Oh now," he said, grinning, the sound echoing in her ears. "Only what you sold to me, of course."

"I never promised you my soul," Lilith spat, anger boiling to the surface.

"Oh, sweetheart. I beg to differ." said the Devil.

Lilith writhed as she sank impossibly deeper. The dank smell of rotten flesh was all around her, inescapable as her feet touched a murky surface.

"Come Lilith and I'll remind you of what you promised me."

He grabbed her hand, a faceless being she could only feel and memories poured through her mind, like reels on a projector.

Please. I only want my revenge. These wolves have laughed in my face, spit on my accomplishments. I want them to know the queen I truly am. Let me have my revenge on them. Let me see them grovel and I'll forever serve you.

Remembering the way his fingers had been made into triangles, with his forefingers tapping gently together, the way his pleasant face had been, Lilith wondered what had happened to him. "I'm still the same Lilith. Of that do not worry."

When his face appeared to her, she sighed. He was a
very enigmatic and handsome man. "Your thoughts are
not your own, you know. I can read them like a novel
and you, my dear, have a very dirty mind. Has sex
always been in the forefront of everything you do?"

"No," Lilith said, a soft chuckle escaping. "Not
until I hit puberty anyway. There were so many
handsome men in the world. It was like living at a
buffet. All the food looked lovely, how could I not
sample all of it?"

His laughter came again, scraping her raw with
pain. "You'll have to forgive me," he said soothingly.
"Laughter, mine in particular, makes them writhe in
pain and I rather enjoy that."

"Why are there so many levels here?"

"Mostly to fulfill their fantasies. You see, some of
them, especially those near the surface are so deluded
that they actually think they can escape eternity here.
They claw endlessly, hoping to reach the world in
which you live, to have one more chance to do it all
right. I've been here since my fall and I can tell you that
none of them has made it yet. But, I indulge them if for
nothing more than the entertainment value. The ones in
the middle layers were decent folks in life. They lived
what you'd call good lives. They failed to realize,
however, that it wasn't that which mattered."

"What mattered?" Lilith asked, curious now.

"Nothing," the man said, obviously uninterested in
elaborating. "In the end, nothing matters. Humans will

live forever thinking they can escape this, but in the end, they'll realize there is no escape from this eternity. I rule all after life."

"Well, then give me the chance to have my revenge, to have the life I envision. Let Romeo Traverse and his family suffer for the evil they've done to me."

"Alright," the handsome man said. His smile spread slowly across his face, but never reached his dark, evil eyes. "I like you, Lilith. You're a practical being, one who knows what she wants and will see it through to the end. You have obviously weighed the cost and decided it's worth your soul."

"You have no idea how long I've been waiting for this moment," Lilith said, as if she wasn't conversing with the Devil himself.

"Oh, but I do. Trust me. It'll be everything you've dreamed of."

Lilith had the sneaking suspicion that the man in the nice suit was lying, but she didn't challenge him. "Thank you," she said adding a smile for charm.

"Don't thank me yet," he grinned. "You don't know how it is that I take a soul from a body."

"Should I be worried?"

"Not really," he exclaimed. "Indulge me, won't you?"

"Sure," she said, knowing she wasn't really in a place to deny him.

"In your world, how depraved is sexuality?" he said with a pointed arch of his brow.

"Well there are your holy-rollers, we'll call them, who believe sex was designed for marriage and outside of that it's a sin. Then you have those who are in monogamous relationships without being married, both heterosexual and homosexual couples. It can get extremely depraved if you delve down into pedophiles," Lilith said, stopping when he held up a hand.

"Oh," he chuckled. "I bet that grates on the nerves of a lot of folks huh? The innocent children? Don't they realize that even children aren't innocent? Children lie, cheat and steal just like their older counterparts. Take a child who's raised in a *good* home and leave the discipline alone for a little while. Let that child learn for himself and I can guarantee you that he will lie, cheat and/or steal by the age of seven. You don't have to teach them, it's innate to their nature."

"Parents often discipline their children for such acts," she said, feeling the need to remind him.

"With little result," he added dryly. "I want you to sacrifice a child to me, a newborn infant, one that isn't what you are."

"You mean a human baby?"

"Yes, now that you mention it," he laughed. "I want a purely human infant sacrificed to me in exchange for what you requested. Your soul will be attached to that baby and I'll give you exactly what you asked for."

Lilith sat back, shocked at the price he asked. She'd considered taking one of the Traverse-Duscene twins if need be to make them suffer. But to snatch a baby from its cradle while its parents slept was another level altogether. "I can't do it," she sighed, defeated. "I can't snatch a newborn baby just to kill it."

"Weak constitution?" he said with elation, radiating pain down her nerves with his laughter so that her body shook as if she'd been tased. "Alright, then take the lives of the Duscene twins. Make it vicious, Lilith or your dreams will fizzle and I'll still have your soul."

"Why children, if you don't mind my asking?"

"What better way to drag their parents down into my realm? Children might be the future of the human race, but in my world they are the key to ruling the human heart. Now wake!"

Chapter Fourteen

Sarina woke to the cries of her sons, startled by a dream that turned her stomach sour. When Brody woke next to her, she didn't shush him back to sleep as she normally did. The hair on her neck stood on end and chills ran down her spine as she crept closer to her sons' cribs. Through the light of the nearly full moon, she could see them sleeping soundly and sighed with relief. She turned to hug Brody and screamed.

The next instant a hand cracked her across the face so hard that her vision blurred. "Shut up, whore!" came a malicious voice. "I took your children the first time and allowed them to live for your father's sake. I won't make the same mistake twice." Sarina watched with tears rolling down her eyes as Lilith approached her babies as they cried. She shushed them, rocking them gently until they went back to sleep.

It was the last thing Sarina saw before that massive hand hit her again, sending her spiraling down into the black abyss of unconsciousness.

"Hello, Sarina." She looked up to see that woman who always emanated a glowing light.

"Hello," she said, smiling. "I didn't realize I had an appointment with you again so quickly. The last time was lovely, thank you."

"We don't have much time this time around I'm afraid. Your children's lives depend on how well you can listen and learn."

"My children's lives? I don't understand." Doubt crept into Sarina's mind as the safety of her children came back to her slowly.

"Lilith, the vampire-wolf from your reality has sought the Devil's help in exacting revenge on your families. The price is the lives of your sons. They are already in peril and only you and yours have the power to save them."

Sarina wanted to cry, but held them back with a determined shake of her head. "Tell me what to do," she said.

"Your mother built the room you used to be a place of relaxation and beauty. However, it can be used for other purposes as long as it's cleansed first. Have her cleanse the room and then take the one you trust most into that room and find your sons. Only in this way can you save them. If you deviate from this, your sons will die."

"But how do we find them?" asked Sarina.

"Use what you know of Lilith, for she is as much a creature of habit as you or me. She'll go where she feels most secure. There, you'll find your boys and through the portal your mother made, you can save them. It's the only way and she won't be expecting it."

"But if you know what she did, doesn't it stand to reason that she'd know what we're going to do?"

"Not in time to stop you," the woman said, her voice deceptively calm. "Now wake!"

"Come on, Sarina. Come back to me, sweetheart."

Sarina woke and coughed violently, turning on her side as her stomach rolled. Turning back she rested for a moment before her eyes, dark and dangerous, met Brody's. "We have work to do."

"I know," he said. "I've already informed everyone in the house. They're getting ready to leave for the caves beyond the woods."

"No," Sarina said, letting Brody help her up. "It must be you and me, only."

"What?" he asked.

"I've received instruction from the woman who's come into my life during the time of need more than I'd care to admit. But I trust what she's told me and I need you to trust me now," said Sarina.

"Alright," Brody agreed. Sarina didn't know if he was being supportive or placating, but she didn't have time to find out either. "Tell me what you need."

"Mother," Sarina said, turning to see the woman who'd given her life. Love swamped her for the maternal bond they shared. "I need you to cleanse the room you made."

"Okay," Amanda said. "I don't suppose you can elaborate?"

"Did you know that it's a portal in this world?"

"I suspected, although I've never used it as one," said Amanda.

"Brody and I must use it to save our sons."

"Then I'll get started now." Amanda's hands trembled in a way that worried Sarina. Pulling Brody into another room, she sighed and ran her hands over her face before she spoke.

"The woman told me that it had to be the person I trust most that did this with me. That's you, hands down, but I need to tell you everything she said." Sarina accepted his embrace as she spoke, feeling comforted in a way only Brody could make her feel. She told him of the entire experience and was thankful when he didn't let her go.

"Then we'll do as she says and send that harpy to hell where she belongs," Brody said, pressing a kiss to Sarina's hair. Feeling unsettled in a way he hadn't in quite a while, not even when the boys had been taken the first time, Brody held Sarina for a long while, as they waited for Amanda to finish with the room.

Two hours later, she came upstairs. "It's done," she said, looking worn through.

"Mother," Sarina said, pulling Amanda into a tight hug. "Get some rest now." Power rippled down Sarina's arm as she squeezed her mother's hand and Sarina watched as Amanda all but fainted. Thankfully, Brody had been there to catch her and after laying her on the bed to rest, the pair headed downstairs.

Brody watched as Sarina opened the door to the room where they'd last made love. Now it was pitch black though, so much so that he couldn't see his hand in front of his face. Reaching out, he found Sarina's hand and held it tight. Then a light so bright that it stung his corneas suddenly lit the room. "You have little time. Use it well," came a soothing, but urgent voice.

When the light dimmed, Brody turned to Sarina. "I'm assuming you know what we have to do?"

"There's a portal here that will open to receive us so that we can pass to wherever the boys are. We're to grab them and come back through the portal. Then it must be destroyed," said Sarina.

"What stops her from trying again?"

"She sold her soul," Sarina said, her eyes looking sorrowful. "She'll die when this is done and her soul will be savagely separated from her body. We'll find her body and destroy it and her soul will suffer for eternity."

"Let's do it then," he said, stepping further into the room. When he reached out though, his hand touched a solid wall. "How do we?"

"I chose you Brody, because I trust you implicitly. You must trust me with the same measure of boldness," said Sarina.

"I do," he said, coming to stand beside her again.

"The power I used on my mother has been there for a while now. I never mentioned it because I didn't want her to feel outdone by her own daughter. Whatever she passed to me through birth is rich, full and beautiful. But it comes with a price. I need to use this power on you."

"Okay," he said. "I trust you, Sarina."

Brody watched her as she started to disrobe and found her impossibly gorgeous. His hands ached to touch her, to draw her close so his body could feast on her flesh. Somehow though, he managed to stand stock still, knowing that whatever she was doing required more from him than just hormones.

"We both need to be naked," she said, her beautiful green eyes were glowing with a heat that nearly seared his skin. Brody quickly disrobed, not bothering to hide his erection. Her eyes never left his face as she took his hand and faced the wall he'd touched earlier.

He watched as she touched the wall with her hand, except now, it rippled like water and the black began to travel up her arm, spreading over her like a liquid curtain. "Sarina," he said as that curtain began to cover her entire body.

"Trust me," she whispered, just before the black covered her mouth. Brody watched it spread up his own arm, amazed at the heat that shimmered over him. It didn't burn him, but it kept him warm. As it covered his face, Brody inhaled deep, afraid he'd have to hold his breath. When it finally reached his other hand and spread out over his fingertips, he felt his body nearly liquefy and suddenly he was standing in a dark, musty smelling cave.

Chapter Fifteen

"We need to move fast!" said Sarina.

Brody looked at Sarina, who seemed much more recovered than he felt. The ringing in his ears echoed back to him as if the walls of the cave could hear it as well. Pointing to his ears, he motioned that he didn't understand.

"The babies are this way," Sarina said. Finally the ringing abated and Brody followed Sarina, trusting that she knew what to do. "Make the change."

Brody did as she asked, taking in the breathless pain as his human shape shifted to that of his wolf. It was never an easy transition. The wolf, dominant in nature, wanted to be done with it as quickly as possible and as bones snapped and lengthened, elbows and knees broke to bend backwards, bones in his nose and mouth grew out from his former jaw. Brody embraced the change, knowing it'd hopefully save his boys and get them all back to the portal alive.

Brody halted when Sarina's hand landed softly on his coat. He sat, turned his head toward her and grinned inside himself, as the human nature tucked away in the wolf, ached to devour her. Still naked, she radiated an inner light that enraptured him. She leaned close to him to whisper in his ear. "The boys are in there. I just don't know how many of them are in there as well. Don't leave my side, okay?"

Taking pleasure in the task, he licked her jaw, smearing slobber halfway up her face. He could have just whined lightly to let her know he understood, but licking her satisfied the man as well and both he and the wolf were laughing. Her hand left his coat and touched the wall of the cave where their twins were. He noticed the way the light around her shimmered and then there was an ear piercing screech that made his ears ring so badly that he could hardly walk. Coming around the corner, he noticed the way the other wolves cowered as Sarina walked into the room. She picked up the boys, cuddling them for a moment.

"Thank you," she said simply and turning, she and Brody were confronted by a band of wolves that weren't prone to her outward show of force. Clutching the twins tightly, Sarina stepped behind Brody who stood to his full height, growling menacingly at the three smaller dogs. The first one, clearly the leader, leapt up, managing an aim that sunk his teeth into the flesh on Brody's shoulder and his resulting yelp of pain shook Sarina from her state of shock. She watched him shake off the first wolf only to have the other two take its place. Sarina could see his struggle to defend her and the twins. It was a terrifying choice, to choose between holding her twins and helping her mate. Setting the twins near her on the floor, Sarina called on the power inside her to aid the man she loved. Seeing them in her mind, Sarina sent short bursts of lightning shooting from her hands.

The two wolves fell away, yelping as they licked the spots where they'd been injured. The leader started to come back at Brody who'd rallied to protect her and their sons. Needing to end this scrimmage so they could make it back to the portal, Sarina used her telepathy to ask Brody to shield the twins. Stepping away from them, she called the lightning to her, letting it soak her skin so that bolts radiated over her body. Then she shot repeating bolts of energy at the three wolves. Grabbing a metal pole that lay close to the table she stood by, Sarina stood it on its end and charged the pole so that it repeated the charges at the three wolves as she'd done. Then, like a switch, Sarina turned off the electrical charge and scooped her boys off the floor.

She fought the fatigue that swept through her like quick-sand and ran with Brody back toward the portal. She knew once she was out of sight, the pole would stop working and the wolves would be on their trail again. "Run," she said to Brody, who instinctively put himself between the three who were pursuing them and her.

Finally the portal came into view and Sarina wasted no time taking her boys through. This time when she touched the wall, it became part of her so quickly that she was engulfed in it before she even knew what had happened. Then they were back home and Brody was changing into his human self. When he reached out to touch the wall, it was once again solid.

"How in the hell did that just happen?"

"I told you that the powers my mother passed to me are full and rich. They're also incredibly amazing."

"How did you?"

"I think I got her powers when she was pregnant with me and Jason. I have no idea if he'd have gotten them as well or if it's just a female, mother to daughter sort of thing. I'm hoping a talk with my mom can add some insight into these new and sometimes scary powers."

"I'm going to get a shower and put some clothes on before I scare someone."

"I'll bring your clothes down. You can use the shower down here."

"Alright," he said. Giving into the need, he pulled her close and while she held their sons in her arms, kissed her soundly. Her soft moan made him thankful that he didn't have to walk through her house with his ass hanging out. A pillow wouldn't have done much to hide his erection at the moment.

He let Sarina lead him out the door and then headed for the shower, thankful all over again that he lived in an era with indoor plumbing. He stepped into the shower and sighed as the hot water soothed the damp that had saturated his flesh, despite being in his wolf. He was shampooing his hair when the shower door opened.

"Mind a little company?"

"Heck no," he chuckled. Closing his eyes, Brody rinsed his hair and yelped when Sarina turned the other faucet on and cold water sprayed his chest. "Hell, Sarina!"

Her giggle rang out as she dipped her dark head under the warm water. Smiling at her, Brody yanked her closer, steadying her when her feet slipped. He caught her around her waist, enjoying the way her beautiful breasts pressed against him. She'd changed physically when she'd been pregnant with the twins. Her stomach had been shoved out of the way to make room for their growing boys and her skin showed the scars they'd left behind. Her breasts, still full from breastfeeding, called to him constantly. Grinning with pure male pleasure, Brody pressed small kisses to the moles that speckled her nearly flawless, cream-colored skin. The pleasure bloomed as her nipples tightened at his touch, satisfying his fingers as they circled those hard tips.

Sarina sighed as Brody tortured her slowly. His hands mastering her body as only he'd ever done. Letting her boys sleep out from under her watchful eye wasn't easy, but in this moment she needed this with Brody, to know that in the light of day, when everything was as normal as it'd ever be for them that they could steal a few minutes to remember that they were more than mother and father. They were mates, soon-to-be husband and wife. She hoped now that things were taken care of as far as Lilith was concerned, that their wedding plans could finally move forward.

By the time they got things done, the boys would be able to walk down the aisle as ring bearers. "You're thinking," Brody whispered as his lips pressed soft kisses over her shoulder. "I'm going to have to ask you to stop doing that for a moment."

"Sorry," she said, giggling. "I just—"

His lips claimed hers in a kiss that seared her soul with the love he carried for her. The force of what she felt for him swamped her and Sarina met Brody with that same measure of love and complete acceptance. If she'd doubted whether or not he was truly the person she trusted most, she knew now there was no one with whom she shared all of herself besides him. Brody was and would always be hers and nothing, she prayed, would ever change that.

As Brody pressed her against the shower wall, Sarina enjoyed the way he touched her, his hands teasing her so that her body wept for their joining. Gone now though was the need for the fast and frenzied finish. He slipped into her slowly, awakening her senses to him. Her body welcomed him deeper as Sarina gave herself up to desire. Each stroke, slow and steady, took her higher. And the need to reciprocate that feeling, urged her to clench her warm pussy around the thickness of Brody's hard cock. Sarina knew next to nothing about men beyond Brody, but somehow, she knew he was perfect for her. She smiled with an inner knowledge of how wonderful it felt to be filled by him. Would he ever know how he pleased her?

Jerking her hips forward, Sarina met Brody's thrust and took him into her fully, feeling the press of his tip against her. Moaning as his mouth suckled her breast, Sarina pulled him closer, the need to be touched by him saturating her. She felt his hands slide up her thighs to cup her ass and whimpered as he filled her over and over again. His mouth claimed hers now, hungry for climax. Their tongues tangled as their bodies pleasured each other and Sarina was flooded by their mutual love as she orgasmed, her body trapping Brody deep inside the hot walls of her tight pussy.

Chapter Sixteen

"We need to find Lilith and destroy her body," Romeo said when they'd all gathered for dinner. The entire pack was still staying on Traverse land, a precaution that would continue until they'd taken out every facet of Lilith and Fenris' army. Romeo knew their forces had been decimated when the Radiants had done their finest work, but it didn't seal the deal for their pack resettling in their homes.

"How can we be sure she's even been stripped of her soul?" asked Brody.

"We can't," Sarina said, grabbing Brody's hand. "But I would think that if she sold her soul, it would be the price to pay, considering she didn't succeed in sacrificing our children."

"What if she was given a deadline and wants to try again?"

"No one's leaving those babies for a minute. We've got around the clock surveillance both inside the house and out. We've got pack members right outside their room and two wolves inside the room at all times. She won't get near those sweet babies again," Amanda said, her own green eyes sharp and deadly serious.

"What if she doesn't need just them? What if it can be any of us as long as we come from the Traverse line?"

"Lilith, for all her faults, isn't dumb," Romeo said, stepping into the conversation. "If she could've chosen any of us, she would have gone after your mother and me, or you and your siblings. Stealing babies, while seemingly easy, simply isn't. Adults will be quiet to spite their captor, babies won't. I'm sure it grated on her nerves that your two little boys cried so much and it's a blessing that you were able to get them in the fashion which you did. I think though, that your mother is right. We have this one chance to destroy her body and we need to take it."

"I just…" Sarina stuttered, looking back up to the room where her boys slept. "I can't leave them."

"Oh, honey," Amanda cooed. "No one is asking you to. You're as much a part of this as anyone, but no one's asking you to leave your sons. You and Brody are both staying here to protect them and this home. Wade, Shawna, and Joshua are all going. Your cousin, Gina, is going to be here though, to keep you company. She can also watch the babies when they're awake."

Sarina smiled then. Gina was just younger than Wade and had come into the world with some complications. Recently moving from abroad and unable to live with her immediate family as they were travelling extensively and had no permanent home for Gina to return to, the Traverse family welcomed her to live with them as one of their own children. She was about to turn twenty-one and although she was stunning like her female cousins, she would never be a breeder. It was something Sarina had envied in her, although times had changed that, especially when Brody entered her world. Born with no detectable reproductive system, Gina took daily hormone shots to keep her system aligned with her anatomy and so far, things seemed solid, although the lack of self-regulated hormones had stunted Gina's growth and she suffered both physically and mentally from it.

"Alright," Sarina said, releasing a pent up sigh of relief. "So what's the plan?"

"We're going to take out Fenris and the rest of his pack. With Lilith gone, I'm sure Fenris isn't fairing too well with the meager wolves he's got left. It shouldn't be overly difficult to dispatch him."

"And," Amanda added. "Once their alpha is gone, the remaining wolves will be given a choice. Join the Delta pack willingly, humbly or die."

Sarina nearly laughed. Her mother was always so to the point about business matters. She could get flustered about the silliest things, but when it came to matters that affected the pack, she was the strongest woman Sarina had ever known. "How will we know it went well?"

"You'll know," Amanda assured her. "Now, get some rest and let Gina help take care of you and your babies. We'll be back before you know it."

<<<◇>>>

"Ready?" Romeo asked, looking at the core of his pack. Over the years, when the children were small, he'd always thought in broader terms when it came to his pack, but now he knew how truly blessed he was to have his children close. His legacy would live on through them, just as he and his siblings carried the weight of their father, Jeremiah's, legacy.

"As we'll ever be," Amanda said, smiling. She stepped closer to him and in a way he'd grown accustomed to, slid her hand into his. He gave it a squeeze and kissed her fully before making the change. When he'd fully turned, she rested that same hand on his back, running her fingers through his coat. He'd never told her how comforting that was. If staying the wolf was as comfortable and sexually fulfilling as being human, he might just consider never changing back, although it'd take her powers to keep him in his changed form for longer than necessary.

Sitting down, Romeo gave a low howl that signaled everyone who'd been briefed to meet at the front entrance. He stepped over to Sarina and Brody, placing a huge paw on his daughter's shoulder. She smiled and stroked his muzzle with affection. Brody grinned and reached behind Romeo's ear for a scratch that made the man inside the beast laugh.

They headed out shortly after that, Romeo leading the way and keeping his other wolves back a good distance. If anything, a trap or entanglement caught him, he didn't want to take any others down with him. Only Amanda walked with him, something he'd never been able to dissuade her from doing. She'd changed since their first heated days of arguments and sex. She'd become immovable on some things, like walking with him when they went about pack business. Whether he was a wolf or a man, she was at his side. Now he considered it a blessing, although he hadn't always seen it that way, particularly when she had carried their children in her womb.

"We're close," she whispered to him, laying a hand on his fur. He twitched to respond and felt that hand slide down his back a few times, her own signal that she'd understood. She stopped and Romeo went ahead a few paces, watching carefully. His eyes scanned the foggy ground and rock crevices before he stepped into the clearing.

Movement caught her eye to the left just before a silver-tipped arrow hit him in the shoulder. He howled both in pain and in warning as another arrow hit him in his hip. Turning, he bolted back into the woods, hot behind Amanda's trail. They reached their pack and Romeo made the change back to the man, cussing as the change only made the pain that much worse. "Let me see," Amanda said, coming to stand beside him once he'd changed.

She knelt down and examined the arrows without touching them. "Neither can be pushed through. They both have bones blocking their progress."

"Terrific," Romeo groaned, pushing a breath of pain past his mouth. "Can you get them out? They're burning the hell out of me."

"Hold on," Amanda said. With a grim face and a toughness he'd taken for granted once upon a time. She braced him against a tree, pressed his arm to his side and yanked the first arrow out. Giving a grunt as she did so, Romeo winced at her.

"Thanks, doll," he said, grinning in relief. Her green eyes met his and Romeo saw a mixture of worry and hunger in those beautiful irises. The hip came next and Romeo nearly fell over in exhaustion after both arrows were out. He examined the tips, careful not to touch them. Made of pure silver, they were expertly crafted. The real question now though, was whether it was a one man show, or whether there were others. Surely Fenris didn't have that many archers left. "Any suggestions?"

"We need to find whoever hit you, make him talk," Wade said, furious in his own right. He'd always been the straight shooter, saying exactly what he meant and standing behind it.

"Agreed," Romeo said, slapping his second oldest son on the shoulder. As a beta, Wade was invaluable to the pack, walking the fine line between the alphas like Jason and Sarina and the omegas like Shawna and Joshua.

Romeo took a few steps away from his pack when he heard a whisper to his right. Turning, he saw a tall, handsome young man. Pushing Amanda behind him, he made the change almost instantly. He let out a low growl before the stranger held up both hands in peace. "I'm not looking for a fight. I was wondering if you might be the Delta pack?"

Curious now, Romeo simply sat down, feeling Amanda step up beside him. "I'm Amanda Traverse, Queen of the Delta pack. This is my husband, Romeo and some of our pack. What can we do for you?"

Romeo could tell the kid was nervous and wondered what he could possibly be so upset about. Then the kid opened his mouth. "My name is Brandt. I… I knew your daughter not so long ago. She helped my wife with the delivery of our twins. I was hoping to thank her and let her know that they are thriving."

"I'm sure she'll be happy to know your babies are faring well," said Amanda.

"Yeah," the man said as his wife stepped up next to him. "This is my wife, Carly."

Romeo watched as he tucked her close to his side and pressed a kiss to her hair, obviously taking care with her. Then Romeo noticed that she was expecting. Before he could make the change and ask the stranger about it, Amanda did so.

"How long has it been since the twins were born?"

"About six months," the man said, obviously worried for his wife. "We weren't aware that she'd get pregnant again so soon."

Romeo watched Amanda step up to the slight woman and smile. "Hi," she soothed. "I'm Amanda. How about we come sit over here and talk for a moment?"

The woman shook her head and Romeo could tell she was having a hard time breathing with the weight of the baby in her womb.

"Romeo, why don't you leave me Shawna and then get on about our business?" asked Amanda.

He stepped over, licked her cheek and then turned toward his pack as Shawna stepped closer to her mother.

"So, you knew my daughter, Sarina?"

"Yes," the man said, not elaborating. Amanda picked up on his nervous twitches and understood there was something or several something's this kid wasn't telling her.

"And she helped you with your twins?"

"Yes," he said, keeping to the one word answers. Amanda could credit her woman's intuition or that of being a mother, but she knew deep down that his man was scared of what would happen if she knew exactly how he'd known Sarina.

"Brandt," she said. "Whatever past you have with Sarina, you two obviously dealt with it. You have nothing to fear from me."

"Is it true that you're a witch?"

Amanda grinned when the question seemed to bubble out from him.

"I am," she smiled. "Although I won't turn you into a toad, if that's what's worrying you."

"No, ma'am," he said. Just then two little boys toddled up next to him, looking very much like their father. Instantly Amanda melted, easily remembering her grandsons who were hopefully home, sleeping. Reaching down, she scooped one of the boys onto her lap while she examined the man's wife.

"I never got a chance to tell your daughter thank you. She helped me when she had every right not to," said Brandt.

"Sarina has always been a headstrong young woman. If she helped you, there was no thanks necessary. I'll tell her you said so though. Where were your sons born?"

"We have a small cottage not too far from here," the man said.

"You're alone out here?"

"I left my pack when I found my wife. She was exiled from her pack and had been wandering for a while. I felt she needed me more than my pack."

"Why didn't you just take her back?" Amanda asked, not showing her surprise at his mention of a pack. Clearly a werewolf, his children would have inherited the gene as well.

"I was afraid that they would have tried to use her as her old pack had. She had several miscarriages before the twins."

"I'm sorry," Amanda said, squeezing the woman's hand. "Well, the good news is that your baby is doing perfectly fine. Your boys are lovely and seem right on track for the little wolves they are. I'm wondering though, if you might like to live in an actual home? We have several empty properties and one I'm sure would be perfect for your family."

"I'm not so sure that'd be a good idea," Brandt replied. "I wasn't exactly nice to Sarina when I knew her. I'm lucky she saw past all of that to help my wife."

"I don't suppose you want to elaborate on that?" asked Amanda.

"Not particularly," he said, his dark eyes regretful. "After I realized I'd played right into Fenris' ploy, I left and never looked back."

"You were part of Fenris' pack?"

"A long time ago. I haven't been there since before the siege on the caves after Sarina was taken."

"How did you know about it if you weren't there?"

"No offense intended ma'am, but your pack doesn't travel lightly and you tromp right past my cottage," said Brandt.

"Where? I've never seen a cottage in these woods."

"Seriously?" he chuckled. "You can't miss it. It's about a thousand yards that way." Brandt raised his arm and pointed in the direction of his cottage.

Amanda looked where the man pointed, but even her keen eyes couldn't pick it out in the dark. "Will you take me there? I'd like to see what you have to work with, should this little darling come when it's just the two of you."

"Certainly," he agreed. He helped his wife up and supported her while the two little boys walked on either side of their parents. Lone wolves or not, they had a beautiful family. Amanda wasn't yet convinced that they shouldn't join the Delta pack. She followed them and was more than a little perturbed when she still didn't see anything.

"Shawna," she called, looking over at her daughter. "You see the cabin he's talking about?"

"If you can call it that. It looks as if there was some work done recently to add more space, but it's barely standing," said Shawna.

Flustered, Amanda tried a quick spell to encourage her vision and still the cabin remained invisible to her. "Okay," she said at last. "Shawna, you're going to have to be my eyes and describe this place to me. I need to know details, things like the number of rooms, approximate size, appliances, etc."

Turning to Brandt, Amanda said, "If I don't deem it suitable, your family will come with me for the time being. I can understand your wanting privacy and all, but your child needs a clean, healthy environment, as does your wife. My husband's pack can provide everything you need to bring this child into the world in an environment that's healthy and full of love and acceptance."

"You don't quite understand," Brandt said, sitting on what must have been steps, not that Amanda could see them. "Please don't kill me for what I'm about to tell you, but I was the man who tricked Sarina into sleeping with me. I'm the man who caused her so much trouble when she was first with Brody. I didn't realize then how I'd played right into Fenris' plans to destroy you."

Amanda had a hard time hearing through the blood that roared through her ears. She closed her eyes tight to fight the urge to turn this man into the toad she'd promised just a little while ago not to. He deserved as much. Then she remembered this man's wife who had been used by wolves who had no sense of family and instantly she knew she had to help them. "My daughter spoke of you only a few times. She was impossibly hurt by your actions and I assume by our last conversation that she's forgiven you. I will also extend forgiveness to you, although you should know that she is my daughter, my firstborn, and I will do whatever it takes to protect her and her family. That being said, I believe she would extend the same invitation to your family. She's sure to love seeing the twins she helped bring into this world and we can always let bygones be bygones."

The man struggled with his decision and kindly asked for a moment to speak with his wife. Amanda pulled Shawna away and asked. "So you really see a cabin there?"

"Yep," she said grinning. "Scary that they brought two little pups into the world in such a rundown shamble of a cottage, but it's there, plain as the nose on my—"

"I get it," Amanda said as she chuckled. "And the nose on your face is plenty plain."

"Hey," Shawna said, pretending to pout. Still, it bothered Amanda that even with her powers, she was unable to see the cottage that was apparently smack dab in the middle of the woods just outside the Delta pack's range.

Chapter Seventeen

"Hello, Lilith," the man with the handsome face said, a pleasant smile on his lips. "I'd welcome you, but you've been here before. You should make yourself at home."

"You took me too early you know," she pouted, trying to hide the real pain that racked her body.

"Oh no," he smiled. "I distinctly remember you asking for time to kill the Duscene twins. You had them in your clutches and lost them still, which I might add, I've watched you do countless times now. Had you sacrificed them the first time, I might have made an exception, but twice you let them slip from your grasp. I'm afraid I can't grant you a third try."

"You don't understand," Lilith wheezed as the pain began to override her ability to talk. "They stole them from me. All I need is one night. I won't take them again. I'll sacrifice them right in the house." Pain radiated along her nerve endings like jolts of electricity, becoming increasingly intense and painful. She whimpered in pain and noticed the gleam in his eyes. "What do they call you here?"

"My subjects?" he chuckled. "They call me God. Up there though, the humans call me all sorts of things.

Satan, The Devil, Evil Incarnate, Hell's Bitch Boy, Master… it all depends on the perspective one uses to get to know me."

"I would guess not too many humans try that."

"Not as many as I would like, but there are other ways to get them over to my side."

"Such as?"

"Ever heard of the apple? The Garden of Eden? It's mostly a myth of legend nowadays. The number of people who think it's bullshit is about equal to those who tote it as truth. I, for one, can tell you without quibbling that it absolutely happened, although it's misinterpreted more than it is spoken of truthfully."

"Then tell me the story," Lilith prompted, suddenly sensing a massive decrease in her discomfort. Breathing easier, she sidled up next to him, sitting at his feet like a child during story time at the library.

"The beginning of the story is always the same. Supposedly, God created this massive, gorgeous garden and stuck two imbecilic humans in it to purportedly rule over all of his other creations. Then along came me and this beautiful Tree of Life. Now Eve, being a woman was much more emotionally driven and not understanding the danger, listened to me. Also, she was incredibly naïve, which helped my argument considerably. All I did was tell her that eating from the Tree of Life would make her like God and boom! Then, without even prompting her, she took the apple to Adam. Adam, not being quite so dunderheaded as his wife, scolded her, but as human men are want to do, he ate of the apple to protect his wife and sentenced himself to exile along with her."

"And?" Lilith urged.

"So you like this story, do you?" he chuckled. "Alright. After they were tossed from the garden, life wasn't nearly as easy as it had been. The thing they didn't quite realize was the punishment they'd accepted upon eating the forbidden fruit. I know most humans often wonder why the Tree of Life was put in the garden in the first place if God knew they would eat off it when He told them not to. Like any father of decent moral standing though, he wanted to test their devotion to him. Just as a parent might set out money to see if their child takes it without asking, God put a tree in the garden to see if Adam and Eve would keep from eating its fruit. It sort of stunk for the serpent, but it sucked even worse for the human race."

"So what's your ending to the story?"

"My story hasn't ended yet and only began that day, but I'll have my time as I'm rather enjoying myself right now."

"No need to conquer mankind?"

"Oh, not entirely. They do a pretty good job of offing each other. Cain killed his brother Abel out of jealousy, an inconsequential emotion. Give humans long enough and they'll often find a way to kill each other. By big numbers as with war, or by small ones like individual murder… it doesn't particularly matter.

Although war often does fill my proverbial coffers. So, are you ready to see where you'll be staying?"

"Not particularly," Lilith replied. As the man stood, the pain came back in waves, making it nearly impossible for Lilith to do anything but scream. As she walked with him down to a staircase below his alter, the pain only grew in intensity. Heat, unlike anything she'd ever felt, overrode her senses and still she walked near him. It was like being burnt alive, except her flesh remained intact, without so much as a scrape or scar.

"I make a very special place for humans who sell me their souls. Now, your pain level will only get worse the further we go down, mainly because it excites me. There's absolutely nothing I love more than to see humans in agony. The louder you scream, the better."

"Why?"

"Why?" he said, laughing. "Why not, darling? I rule here and as the supreme God, I will have my way."

"The Bib—" Lilith found a massive hand around her throat and it squeezed until she was coughing harshly, desperate for air she couldn't draw in. The man's face had turned hideous, which compounded Lilith's fear for her fate.

"You'll never say that word to me. I have a severe abhorrence to words that equate me to that book of lies. I'll not be spoken to of it or anything related to it. Do you understand?"

Tears rolled down her cheeks as Lilith nodded in agreement. "Get those thoughts out of your head, girl. You were marked for me the moment you sold your soul to me. There is no redemption of any kind for the likes of you."

The man who'd once had a handsome face turned away and was gone in an instant, leaving Lilith to writhe in pain next to millions of other people who'd apparently sold their souls to him as well.

Sarina checked on her sons for the fifteenth time in as many minutes, smiling when she saw them sleeping. Tucked into their beds soundly, she turned and greeted the two guards who'd just switched shifts. They sat in silence. She knew they took time away from their own families to help protect hers. She told them of her gratitude before she stepped out. At the door outside of the boys' room inside her parents' home, she greeted two other guards. They stood in silence as well, ready to her sons. "Thank you," she said before heading downstairs.

Sarina found Gina and Brody in the dining room playing gin rummy while munching on nachos.

"What a dinner," she said with a grin, bending down to kiss her husband.

"Ew," Gina said, rolling her eyes.

"Just wait little cousin." Sarina gave her a smile. "You'll catch a man's eye someday soon and be swept off your feet as well."

"Please," Gina said, her lisp tripping up her *s* sound. "No man is going to want me. I can't breed like you and Shawna."

"Well maybe you should step out and look at a man who isn't a werewolf like us. I'm sure there's a man out there who'd find you to be his dream, darling. Be patient."

"Easy for you to say," Gina said, almost pouting.

"Please sweetheart, try to remember, I didn't meet Brody until I was your age. Maybe this is your year."

"Probably not," Gina said. "But I'm about to stomp your man in gin rummy so it's good."

"She's a shark," Brody said with a smile. "She'd got me up to a hundred. At this rate we'll be broke and living back here with your parents."

"Nah," Sarina said with a grin. "You'll get her."

"Not likely," said Gina. "Gin." She smacked the cards down on the table and raised her arms in a victorious stance.

"See?" Brody said, quirking an eyebrow up at his wife.

"Well it goes to a good cause. Maybe we'll start a *Find Gina a Man Fund*," Sarina teased, tossing her cousin's hair. She felt for her. At twenty-four, Gina was blossoming into the spitting image of her mother and was smart enough to know that she wouldn't be wanted by a man who could shift into a wolf. Sarina made a mental note to speak with her mother about introducing Gina to some human men. There was no reason she couldn't find a husband, given her unique situation.

<<◇>>

Sabrina knew instinctively that her family would be out over the long night, but she still found it hard to sleep. Ever since getting the boys back, she preferred to take turns with Brody, alternating four to six hour shifts so that one of them was always up to help keep watch. Until someone proved to her that Lilith really was in the pits of hell and Fenris was dead as well, she'd keep a mother's vigil over her sons. It was her most important job and she'd do it expertly.

"Get some sleep," Brody whispered, pressing a warm kiss to her neck. "I'll keep watch now."

Sarina snuggled down into the covers of their bed, feeling the warmth from where Brody had left it just minutes ago. She slipped into sleep peacefully, thankful for a dreamless sleep for the first time in a while. Still, she knew deep down that the peaceful feeling she had wouldn't last. It never did, especially where her family was concerned. Someone or something would always hunt them and she hoped, prayed that it wouldn't be the son of man. That'd make it increasingly hard to hide themselves amongst them if it ever turned to war between their kind and humankind.

-To be continued in Book 4-

If you enjoyed this title, I would appreciate your leaving a review of the book. Good reviews encourage an author to write as well as help books to sell. Good reviews can be just a few short sentences describing what you liked about the book without having a spoiler. If you could spend 30 seconds writing a review, I would appreciate it: you can review this title right now at your favorite retailer.

Here is a preview of the **next story** you may enjoy:

Alpha Strategy: Romeo Alpha Blood Lines Romance, Book 4

ROMEO TRAVERSE waited just outside the woods, his shoulder and hip still ached from the silver-tipped arrows his wife, Amanda, had removed less than four hours before. His pride, however, would take longer to heal. As the alpha of the Delta pack, taking two arrows in battle scored him deeper than the tips could ever hope to penetrate. Still, he had his beautiful wife to thank for the healing that was already working its magic. Without it, he'd never have gotten this far. Still in his wolf, Romeo sat scanning the tree line. He'd brought everyone from his pack who'd been available to help. Gina, his niece, had stayed behind with Sarina, her older cousin and his first born. Brody, Sarina's husband, had also stayed behind with four soldier wolves to guard his two grandsons. As the youngest heirs to the Delta pack, Jedidiah and Brody Jr. couldn't be risked and with one attempt already foiled to use them as bait, Romeo wasn't about to take another chance with them by removing their father. He'd spared the four wolves without hesitation.

His middle son, Wade, had made the trip as had his two youngest twins, Shawna and Joshua. Shawna was a ways back in the wooded area of their territory helping her mother take care of two wolves who'd come from somewhere in the woods. How they'd missed their presence all this time was a concern for another day as Romeo waited.

The arrows that had sunk into his flesh had come from the direction that Romeo was now exploring and he would find the shooter. As for whether or not that shooter was alone, well, he'd just have to figure that out along the way. And figure it out he would. The safety of his entire pack depended on ending Fenris once and for all.

Sitting on his haunches to breathe for a minute, Romeo thought back to all they'd gone through; the very first werewolf had a penchant for ruling everything.

Thankfully, the Delta pack had rallied and come back even stronger after Fenris and his pack had wiped out several of the male wolves' families. Nearly a hundred women and children had died that night and it had crippled Romeo's numbers, not to mention what it had done to the pack's morale. Over the last few months, Romeo and his entire family had worked themselves to the bone to keep those male wolves from defecting and going after Fenris on their own. He was glad to have all of them with him tonight. Three nights away from the full moon, he needed every wolf he could get for this fight, especially if he was going to end it once and for all.

The arrows he'd received were a precursor, he knew, to what was coming. Fenris had wolves under his command who'd take on the fight and keep going. Romeo could only hope that Fenris didn't have enough. If any other packs came to join him, Romeo knew it'd be bloody and brutal, something he wanted to avoid at all costs. He wasn't afraid of the fight, but he didn't want to waste the lives of his pack members just to snuff out a wolf who should have died eons ago... one who'd caused more than his fair share of trouble. The mere fact that he'd planted a decoy, a wolf who'd disguised himself as Sarina Traverse's own mate, Brody, galled Romeo more than he wanted to admit. And to think that worthless black magician Dankar had been able to pull off such a ruse.

Romeo knew better than anyone that war was personal, from the infantry all the way up to the decision makers. Just as he knew that Fenris had more than overstepped his bounds when that young man had done his dirty deed. He wasn't one to hold a grudge, but in Fenris' case, he'd certainly make an exception. And as if Fenris wasn't enough to deal with these past months, they'd had to put up with Lilith, the woman who created the werewolves in the first place. It pricked his ego considerably to have to admit that she had duped him. Consumed by black magic, she'd found a way to crawl back from the pits of Hell and somehow managed to slither inside Brody's mind. It wasn't long before she'd found her body. It had cost Romeo his son and now he owed Fenris for Jason's death as well.

"Sir."

Romeo turned to see one of his generals standing at his side and quickly put away thoughts of the past. He tilted his head and the man continued

"Your scouts have returned with a count."

Romeo knew the change would hurt and likely drain his energy even more, but he also knew that he needed to get the information correct the first time around. It took mere minutes for the shift to complete and Romeo was thankful for the young man who tossed him a pair of shorts to put on.

"What's the report?" Romeo asked, knowing they needed to formulate a plan of attack that would end Fenris' pack forever.

"There's some twenty-five archers posted around the area sir. Some I recognized but plenty I didn't. I don't mean to assume sir, but I'm almost sure Fenris has asked for and received outside help. He's never been dumb in the past and I doubt he'd slip up now, sir."

"Thank you," Romeo said, dismissing the young man with a wave of his hand. The young scout took his original place in the pack and Romeo turned to his top four wolves. "Alright, obviously we need these wolves taken out before we see about attacking the wolves inside the caves. None of us here have been inside, save me, and that will need some attention to detail. Right now though, I want our archers to worry about the twenty-five wolves that our scout saw. That's Fenris' front line of defense and that's where we'll strike first."

If you enjoyed this sample then look for **Alpha Strategy: Romeo Alpha Blood Lines Romance, Book 4**.

Here is a preview of **another story** you may also enjoy:

Romeo Alpha: A BBW Paranormal Shifter Romance - Book 3

ROMEO FELT groggy as he surveyed his surroundings. The last thing he could remember was saying his vows to the love of his life, Amanda, and then he must have passed out. He was sore all over, and he realized he was tied to a post of some kind. The chill of the wind and the lightness of the atmosphere told him that he was high up in the trees on one of the many mountains near his home, but where was Amanda? Was she all right? Who had tied him up?

He looked down at his shoulder which was aching and saw that a piece of silver was buried deep inside his skin, creating a painful wound. If he could get it out, he could shift if need be. But he would have to get out of the binds that held him first.

Then, squinting in the dark, he saw a figure approaching him. He was about to get his answer. A fire crackled nearby, and he craved the warmth, though he'd prefer the warmth of his bride next to him instead.

"Well, well, look who's awake."

Romeo recognized the voice, and the flames revealed a familiar face. "Remus, what in the hell is going on here? Untie me right now! My mate could be in danger."

"Oh, my friend, I knew this was going to be fun, but you're making it even better for me." Remus' evil grin sent a shiver down Romeo's spine. He pulled something from his jacket, and Romeo froze. "What, you aren't so brave now when you're facing silver bullets? You know, fear isn't going to save you. You see, you've been put entirely in my charge for now. And unless the mate you speak of does as she is told, I get to kill you. As it is, I get to torture you and maim you."

He shot at Romeo; once, twice, three times, burying bullets into his flesh. They hit his arm and his leg in quick succession. Romeo gritted his teeth and tried not to show how much pain he was in. The silver was searing his flesh, ripping through his body. The fire surged through him, and his head felt like it was going to explode. Any hope of shifting and getting out of this mess was gone.

"Damn it, Remus. You used to be one of us. I know you care for Audri and she cares for another, but this is no reason to betray your own kind. What could possibly be in it for you? And where is my mate, my bride? It sounds like you know." Romeo commanded the strength of the alpha to sound as menacing as possible, but he had a feeling Remus was too far gone. This was not the child who had followed his little sister around like a lost puppy dog. This was an evil man looking for blood.

"I'm in it for Audri, of course. She was promised to me if I successfully kept you here until your mate completed the task she was given. You see, I chose to align myself with someone more powerful than either of you could ever hope to be. He will give me everything I wish for. In the end, your stubborn sister will bow at my feet and beg for me to have her."

"Where is Amanda?" Romeo's voice echoed through the dark night, causing Remus to jump a little. Romeo smiled; but Remus shot him with another silver bullet. It hit his knee cap, going through the joint. Romeo screamed out in pain, no longer able to control it.

"Your precious Amanda is probably making her way to Dean right now to give up her powers. It is the only way she is allowed to have you and the other Radiants back, though I may take one of those Radiants for myself."

Romeo was disgusted by the man who was once a friend, the man who might have once had a chance at being his brother-in-law. "I was going to have Amanda, but you have rendered her useless to me, now. The damn mating ritual made it so I can't pleasure her even if I wanted to. Not that any of it matters now. I will have your damn pack anyway once you and your stupid brother are out of the picture."

Romeo couldn't help but chuckle. "I thought part of the plan was to keep me alive. It'll be you who's dead if you go against your orders. Besides, you are no match for me or my wife. She has more power than you could even imagine, and I doubt she'll give it away to that evil man who calls himself her brother. She'll have a plan."

"For your sake, you better hope not, Romeo, because that will certainly mean your death. And I will show no mercy. You will suffer greatly if you die directly at my hand. Now, get some rest. I'm sure you'll need your strength, since you'll be back to procreating with your mate and wife by this time tomorrow night. Though, I'm not sure you'll still want her once she's practically a human. Of course, that's if Dean let's her live. He can be testy, that one. You better pray she keeps her trap shut."

Remus turned to walk away from Romeo, but Romeo pulled a pocket of phlegm from the back of his throat and launched it at Remus. It landed on his cheap Goth boots.

Remus turned around with a snarl. "I said it was time to rest, Romeo, but then again, you never did listen. How does it feel to be pulled off your god-like pedestal and learn you're no better than anyone else?" Remus didn't wait for an answer. He kicked out his boot, the same one Romeo had landed the wad of spit on, and kicked Romeo square in the head. Romeo's world went pitch black as he was knocked into a dreamless sleep.

If you enjoyed this sample then look for **Romeo Alpha: A BBW Paranormal Shifter Romance - Book 3**.

Here is a preview of **another story** you may also enjoy:

Devil's Advocate: A BBW MC New Adult Romance Series - Book 3 by Carla Coxwell

THE POPPING noise echoed so loudly that Kristie had to cover her ears. The sudden pain in her abdomen made her nauseous. Surprised, Kristie looked down and saw red soaking through her T-shirt. She looked up, panicked, and saw a cloaked figure running away…

Kristie's eyes opened and she lurched upward, breathing hard. She clawed at her belly, trying to get the red off, when she realized that she wasn't on the sidewalk, staring down into the cloaked face of the man who had shot her. No, Kristie was in her apartment with Gray snoring next to her.

Gray, she thought, turning to look at him. She felt covered in sweat, sticky and warm on her body from her nightmare. Always the same nightmare. The morning she had been shot, always a little different than how it actually happened. Kristie rubbed her brow, trying to wipe the sweat off, but her hand was clammy. Gray didn't stir.

Kristie had hoped that Gray would wake up. Maybe somehow sense that she had been having her same nightmare again and hold her. Almost in response, Gray let out a loud snore and shifted onto his back. A nightlight in the corner illuminated the room in a soft glow. Gray had thought it was silly, Kristie knew, when she had suggested putting them around their apartment. But he hadn't made fun of her. He understood.

The fear that Kristie had lived with since she had woken up in the hospital six months ago, after being gunned down due to the gang battle Gray was involved in, came rolling over her. She gripped her stomach, feeling sick, remembering the pain of being shot. It was silly to even be thinking about it. But if Kristie allowed herself, she could still vividly recall those few seconds right before the gun had gone off.

Kristie squeezed her eyes tightly. No, not right now. The clock near her side of the bed showed it was four in the morning. She slid out of bed, nervous about heading toward the kitchen alone to get water. *Get over it*, she lectured herself, always harder on herself than anyone else was. Six months since being shot twice and almost dying. Was she supposed to be over it already? She asked herself those questions almost daily and never had an answer.

The coolness of the tiles in the kitchen helped steady her a bit. Kristie got a glass of water and drank it slowly, looking at the nightlight over the counter, which was brighter than the others. Gray joked that it was almost as if the lights were on. Kristie didn't care. It was silly, because it hadn't even been dark when she had been shot. But the darkness now felt imposing, as if it hid a million enemies, all coming after her.

Recovering after being shot had been difficult. Kristie had lost a lot of blood from the two life-threatening bullets. She had been in the hospital for almost a month recovering. Gray had sworn that Armand had been the one who had fired the gun, or hired the person to fire the gun – either way, Gray blamed Armand. Kristie didn't know who it had been.

All she knew was that it had been part of the gang violence that Gray swore he wouldn't fall back into.

But Gray hadn't removed himself from it. He said it was because he wanted to avenge her. As Kristie took another sip of water, all she could think was that she didn't want to be avenged. She hadn't died. She wanted to live with Gray and start their married life with a new baby. That was all Kristie could think about lately. Having a baby and raising a baby. That would bring Gray back to Earth and give him something to truly care about. It was what Kristie wanted as well.

She finished her water and rubbed her eyes, sighing. If Kristie stayed up like this, she'd be over-thinking everything. *I need to go to bed.* She had work in the morning and couldn't be replaying the last year in her mind any longer. Kristie turned around and headed back to bed. She walked a little quicker than she would have in the daylight.

Gray wiped his hands on his pants, trying to get some of the car grease off of them. Rick was strolling toward him, puffing on a cigarette. It seemed impossible, but Rick had actually grown bigger in the last six months. He looked like a gladiator or something, Gray mused as he walked out of his uncle's garage.

"There you are," Rick said. "I have to get the oil changed in Kass's car and wouldn't mind seeing you actually do some work for a change."

Gray laughed. "Hey, I do plenty here."

Rick wrinkled his nose as if he didn't quite believe him. "I'll admit it – thought you could give me a discount, too."

"I'll see what I can do," Gray said, pretending to consider it.

"Thanks, pal."

"Kass didn't want to drop it off?" Gray asked, heading over to her car.

Rick shook his head. "She had to get to work. I told her I could do it for her. She's trying to catch up on work since she had that cold last week."

Gray nodded, but his thoughts were elsewhere. Rick and Kass had so easily settled into married life. Easier than Kristie and he had. *Kass wasn't shot the morning of their honeymoon though*, Gray reminded himself gently. Maybe if Kristie hadn't been, things wouldn't be as messy as they were now.

Almost as if Rick sensed Gray's thoughts, he asked, "How is Kristie doing?"

Gray shifted his weight, leaning back against Kass's car. "Okay."

Okay about summed the situation up. Kristie had recovered from her life-threatening gun shots from Armand. Gray had sworn to take Armand down for what he had done but it turned out it hadn't been that easy. Armand had gone underground, impossible to find. Gray had been trying to have the asshole show his face so he could blow it off, but he'd had no luck.

Instead, the Infernos had been pressing on them harder, just in ways that were harder to strike back against. Burning the warehouse down and trying to shoot Gray in the face had apparently been their big plans. When both had failed to kill Gray and ruin the Devil's Advocates, they had tried smaller ideas. Trying to frame them for crimes and constantly having the cops on Gray's ass.

All of it had added a lot of stress to his relationship with Kristie. She wanted Gray to leave the gang, like he had said he would do when they married. But that had been before Kristie had been shot. There was no way that Gray could let Armand get away with almost killing her. No matter how much Kristie wanted everything to go back to a pretty, perfect life, Gray couldn't allow Armand to get away with what he had been doing.

"She still afraid of the dark?" Rick asked, breaking through Gray's thoughts.

Gray nodded. "Yeah. Still don't totally understand it, since the shooting happened in the day but…she's doing the best she can."

"She still talking about a kid?"

Gray nodded, falling silent again. Kristie seemed obsessed with the idea of having a child. It wasn't that Gray was against it, *per se*, but he didn't know if now was the best time. They had just moved into their own apartment with the money Gray had made from working at his uncle's garage as well as what he pulled in from the gang. Kristie had gotten a job at a law office doing clerical work and had been discussing going back to school for her law degree.

"It just doesn't feel like the best time to have a kid," Gray finally said.

Rick took a drag off his cigarette. "Never is a good time for one, is it?"

Gray nodded in response as the subject changed back to Kass's car. Things felt so messy. He wasn't sure how to put them back into their proper places.

If you enjoyed this sample then look for **Devil's Advocate: A BBW MC New Adult Romance Series - Book 3 by Carla Coxwell**.

Other Books by Darla Dunbar

- The Romeo Alpha BBW Paranormal Shifter Romance Series (This series precedes the "Romeo Alpha Blood Lines Romance Series")

- The Alpha Feud BBW Paranormal Shifter Romance Series

- The Alpha Packed BBW Paranormal Shifter Romance Series

- The Daemon Paranormal Romance Chronicles

- The Mind Talker Paranormal Romance Series

- The Leather Satchel Paranormal Romance Series

Get the latest update on new releases from the author at:

https://darladunbar.com/newsletter/

About the Author - Darla Dunbar

Darla has been interested in paranormal romance since she was a teenager in high school. It was then that she discovered she could fulfill her fantasies through her writing.

Observing people and human behavior in the area of romance has always been one of her favorite pastimes. Combining that with an overactive imagination is a sure fire way of coming up with interesting themes.

Connect with Darla Dunbar

I really appreciate you reading my book! Here are my social media coordinates:

Friend me on Facebook:
https://www.facebook.com/darladunbar/

Follow me on Twitter: https://twitter.com/DarlDunbar

Check me out on Goodreads:
https://www.goodreads.com/author/show/8425857.Darl
a_Dunbar

Subscribe to my newsletter:
https://darladunbar.com/newsletter/

Visit my website: https://darladunbar.com/

www.ingramcontent.com/pod-product-compliance
Lightning Source LLC
Chambersburg PA
CBHW030756200726
48288CB00004B/1197